Advance, Retreat

Advance, Retreat

SELECTED SHORT STORIES BY
RICHARD RIVE

Woodcut illustrations by
Cecil Skotnes

ST. MARTIN'S PRESS
New York

First published in the United States of America in 1989
Printed in South Africa
ISBN 0-312-03689-2

Library of Congress Cataloging-in-Publication Data

Rive, Richard, 1931–1989
    Advance, retreat : selected short stories / by Richard Rive :
woodcut illustrations by Cecil Skotnes.
        p.   cm.
    Originally published : Cape Town : D. Philip, 1983.
    Contents : Moon over District Six - - Dagga-smoker's dream - - Rain -
- The bench - - Resurrection - - No room at solitaire - - Drive in - -
Riva - - The visits - - Make like slaves - - The man from the board - -
Advance, retreat.
    ISBN 0-312-03689-2
    I. Title.
PR9369.3.R58A6   1989
823- -dc20
                                                                89 - 10636
                                                                        CIP

Contents

FOR CANDICE RUTGERS
With special thanks to
Braam de Vries
who made it all possible

Acknowledgements

The short stories published in this collection have appeared in over twelve different languages in more than twenty-two countries. The journals and anthologies in which they have appeared are too numerous to list in detail. The author, however, wishes especially to thank those in which he first appeared, such as *New Age, Fighting Talk, Black Orpheus* (Nigeria), *Transition* (Kenya), *Argus, Drum* and *Contrast*.

Particular thanks are due also to Cecil Skotnes for kindly offering to illustrate the stories.

Moon over District Six

The moon was recklessly gay and shouted 'Happy New Year' to the stars. The stars twinkled back coyly 'Same to you'. The moon, a crazy whore, did a comic turn around staid, spinsterly Table Mountain and then bounced dizzily across the sky. District Six hopped, skipped and jumped.

The streetlamps laughed as a handful of teasers went streaming red, white and blue down Tennant into Hanover Street.

     Buy my teasers
     See 'em blow in 'e breezes

sang the teaser-man who considered himself a poet. The teaser-man knew it was New Year's Eve. The teasers also knew.

"Dey make me wan' 'e wheezes," laughed a young buck to his girl-friend, proud of his wit. He also thought he might be a poet.

"What's wheezes?" she inquired coyly.

"Wheezes is wheezes. Don't you know *wheezes!*" He made it sound obscene.

"Sis, Boetie!" she said, mustering all the dignity she could. Then she burst out into uncontrollable giggles.

Up Hanover Street streamed the teasers to pause at the fish-market.

"Happy New Year, Merrim," said an early celebrator, pirouetting on the pavement in a paper cap that read KISS ME SWEETIE. In his hand was an empty bottle of Oom Tas which shouted 'Kiss me too'.

"You must learn to control your filthy mouth," said a prim, light-brown lady who lived in Walmer Estate and only spoke English at home.

"Why did 'e white man blame me becaws I'm cuuuuulid . . ." sang an amorous swain serenading an empty lane on his gaudy guitar. The lane displayed no interest but a cheeky, yellow youth looked up momentarily from a pair of dice he was rolling.

"I'm a guy who never done no haaaarm."

"You singing shit!" shouted the cheeky dice-roller.

"Why did the policeman beat me becaws I'm cuuuuulid . . ." sang the imitation Caruso.

"Your mama's bloomers!" shouted the yellow youth spitting on his dice. "Come quick, six's my nick!"

Buy my teasers
See 'em blow in 'e breezes

sang the teaser-man who tried to be original.

"Dere's a fight on 'e corner an' dey buggerin' up yer man!" shouted an urchin with splayed toes to a tired woman with tired breasts.

"Lemme go, he started first!" screamed her man, shielding his face from flying boots.

"Leave him alone!" screamed the woman hysterically, as she attacked his assailant.

"Jeesus, what a helluva lotta blood," whispered the urchin, in awe, to his guttersnipe sister.

Buy my teasers
See 'em blow in 'e breezes

sang the teaser-man who thought it safer to mind his own business.

"Hier ko' die law!" warned a frightened, thin-necked spectator who kept to the outer fringe of the crowd.

"Break it up break it up break it up," said authority in the shape of a white policeman with his hand on his revolver holster.

"To hell with the law!" shouted a voice that preferred to remain obscure in the crowd.

"Who said that!" the brass buttons and revolver holster demanded.

"Happy New Year," replied a jelly-drunk man who had stopped trying to convince everyone that he was sober.

"Believe in the Lord and thou shalt be saved," foamed a street-corner Jesus-jumper.

"Here's a penny for yer collection plate," interjected a skollie who was not interested in his soul. "Buy a drink on me."

"Sinner," raved the bible-thumper, "when the Lord told me to come, I came!"

"Here's anurrer penny. Buy yerself a teaser," said the facetious one.

Buy my teasers
See 'em blow in 'e breezes

sang the mute, inglorious teaser-man.

"Gimme two," said a reckless, highly rouged housewife who had to bribe her kids because she was never at home.

"I say, pal, buy us two for downstairs," said a flashily dressed dandy in pink socks who wanted to jump the cinema queue.

"I'm a'ready buying five tickets," lied a frightened, timid stranger.

"O'y two extra, man," pink socks insisted.

"But I'm a'ready buying five," said the frightened stranger.

"Don' try an' be smart or I'll rip your guts," said pink socks who had no knife. "Better buy it an' don' talk so much."

"A'right," said the very frightened stranger.

"So I says to her, how about a date, honey?" said an under-nourished seventeen-year-old lying about his sexual exploits.

"Honey, t'ink you funny," said an admiring wit.

"In you' bunny," added the third rhymester.

The moon zigzagged crazily across the sky bumping a star or two out of the way, then bounced off Table Mountain. After all it was New Year's Eve and District Six was delirious with joy.

Buy my teasers
See 'em blow in 'e breezes

sang the teaser-man.

Dagga-smoker's Dream

Of course there were times when he had to have it, but this wasn't one of them. Or was it? There were times when the craving gnawed inside him like his longing for Honey, when his world spun round, dragging him down in a whirlpool, spinning and longing, and longing and spinning, and holding on tightly although there was no grip. There were times when the longing grew to a thirst that left his throat parched and raw; that no amount of cheap wine could assuage, so that there remained only the desire to sink away into nothingness, forgetfulness, muddled oblivion which sharpened the appetite instead of reducing it.

Karel wanted to forget, but not merely for the sake of forgetting. He wanted to forget that he had kicked Honey, that he had kicked her insensible, that he had not used fists but feet, that he had kicked until the sole of his shoe glowed with blood — a fascinating red that had made him wish to paint it even redder with sheer brutality. He had to forget, because he did not know why he had kicked her. She had sat on the pavement sipping a Cola and twirling her shoe on the end of a bare toe. And he had called her in and kicked her and kicked.

Grimy steps and dirty bow-legged, pot-bellied children. Neon lights apologising over District Six. Children fascinated Karel when he was drunk or full of dagga. Dirty children with runny noses and spindly legs, and there, leaning against the wall of Seven Steps, the pusher, who recognised him.

Forgetfulness. To forget that he had kicked Honey. Forgetfulness that brought oblivion. Oblivion and one became a man and one was strong so that one could draw breath through the teeth and defy the whole damn world. To buy oblivion wrapped in brown paper.

The noticeboard on the train became difficult to read. S. . .L. . .E. . . and where there should have been a letter there was nothing. Nothing but hysterical laughter at finding nothing. Peals of hysterical laughter because he had a right to kick Honey if she showed her body in the street. Not jealousy but a kind of respectability. Respectability even if she was only one of his women. Well, maybe a little jealousy. Bodies on exhibition and a blur where G should come to spell out SLEGS BLANKES, which meant whites only; which meant running on rubbery legs to the third-class compartment.

A crowded train going God knows where. But then he was going God knows where. And why should he sit even if there were seats? Standing against the door people could see him, could laugh with him, or maybe at him. Maybe see Honey's bleeding face through him. They were his friends at the back of the carriage, that was why they laughed with him. Laughed at Honey. He was popular at the back of the carriage, and everyone getting up and grinning at him. Salt River . . . Plumstead . . . Retreat . . . Plumstead . . . Salt River. What the hell did he care? Everyone staring at him. Everybody but the white man reading a book. Or was it one of those Wynberg upper-class coloureds? Reading a book while he, Karel, was busy entertaining people. And the train jolting. What the hell did he think he was? A white man? Or coloured? And he, Karel, a dagga-smoker. A dagga-smoker who had kicked Honey. Others are looking at me and that white—coloured man ignoring me. Reading a book and ignoring me. He and that girl in front of him.

"Hullo darling?"

Peals of laughter from the back as he sidles next to the girl.

"Leave me alone."

"I'm on'y being friendly, sweetheart."

More laughter.

"Leave me alone."

"I on'y want to touch you. Jy's mos 'ie kwaad 'ie?"

"I ask you to leave me alone."

A long pause broken by the tittering at the back.

"I'm not one of those girls you pick up in Long Street."

"To hell with Long Street. What kin' offa girl are you?"

"Please leave me alone."

"Why, Honey?" The name erupted and retreated dizzily.

"I said leave me alone."

"I'm a coloured man an' you're a coloured girl so what's the difference?"

Then with a leer at the reading man, "Or do you on'y want white men?"

The man skipped a line and then went on reading.

"If you smoke dagga, smoke it for yourself. Now I'm asking you to let me go!"

"You particular, hey, on'y want white men, hey?"

Karel looked around him for his friends and met the eyes of the man staring coldly at him. Karel stared back defiantly and then saw the pleading eyes of Honey. He dropped his eyes in a haze of shame, self-consciousness and pseudo bravado.

"I say, gi' us a kiss, sweetheart."

"Let me go."

"Net een soentjie!"

"Leave me alone, I'm warning you."

"Like hell you are. Won't give a little kiss," he said, grinning slyly at the reading man. No response. Why the hell didn't he open his mouth?

"You can go to hell. I don't want you for no girl-friend any more."

"I'm not your girl-friend. Let me pass." She appealed to the ticket examiner.

"It's all right. It's on'y my sweetheart, guardjie. Having a little quarrel."

"I don't know him. Let me pass, I'm telling you!"

"Komaan, laat haar verby. Jy's weer vol boom, nê?"

"Awright, guardjie. No offence meant. All forgotten. So long, sweetheart."

She gathered up her bag and made for the next compartment.

Karel shook his head and tried to focus his eyes. She had left. He felt that Honey had walked out on him again. Sipping a blooming Cola. He felt eyes on him. That bastard who was reading. What was he doing in a third-class comparment? Now swells of humiliation and self-pity. He must do something to regain his self-respect. Show that man that he was Karel. Keep those at the back laughing with him.

"To hell with you all on the train."

No response other than fresh peals of laughter.

"I'm born in District Six in 'e Mokkies Buildings in Tennant Street and I'm prepared to knock the hell outta everyone here."

A pathetic figure with pupils hanging low in the eyes. Karel drunk with power because his oaths go unchallenged.

"Those blerry upper-class types who can't afford to sit first class. They can sit where they bloomingwell like. Third class belongs to us. They must clear out!"

Spume fluttering.

"I'm not afraid of anyone! black or white! I'm born in District Six!"

Plumstead . . . Retreat. The man shut his book and got up.

Karel clambered over a passage and amid raucous laughter proceeded to open all the windows.

Rain

Rain pouring down and blotting out all sound with its sharp and vibrant tattoo. Dripping neon signs reflecting lurid reds and yellows in mirror-wet streets. Swollen gutters. Water overflowing and squelching onto pavements. Gurgling and sucking at storm-water drains. Table Mountain cut off by a grey film of mist and rain. A lost City Hall clock trying manfully to chime nine over an indifferent Cape Town. Baleful reverberations through a spluttering all-consuming drizzle.

Yellow light filtering through from Solly's 'Grand Fish and Chips Palace'. Door tightshut against the weather. Inside stuffy with heat, hot bodies, steaming clothes, and the nauseating smell of stale fish oil. Misty patterns on the plate-glass windows and a messy pool where rain has filtered beneath the door and mixed with the sawdust.

Solly himself in shirt sleeves and apron, sweating, vulgar and moody. Bellowing at a dripping woman who has just come in.

"Shut 'e damn door. You live in a tent?"

"Ag, Solly."

"Don't ag me. You coloured people never shut blarry doors."

"Don't you bloomingwell swear at me!"

"I bloomingwell swear at you, yes."

"Come. Gimme two pieces o' fish. Tail cut."

"Two pieces o' fish."

"Raining like hell outside," the woman said to no one.

"Mmmmmm. Raining like hell," a thin befezzed Muslim cut in.

"One an' six. Thank you. An' close 'e door behin' you."

"Thanks. Think you got 'e on'y door in Hanover Street?"

"Go to hell!" Solly cut the interchange short and turned to another customer.

The north-wester sobbed heavy rain squalls against the windowpanes. The Hanover Street bus screeched to a slithery stop and passengers darted for shelter in a cinema entrance. The street lamps shone blurredly.

Solly sweated as he wrapped parcels of fish and chips in a newspaper. Fish and Chips. Vinegar? Wrap. One an' six please. Thank you! Next. Fish an' chips. No? Two fish. No chips? Salt? Vinegar? One an' six please. Thank you! Next. Fish an' chips?

"Close 'e blarry door!" Solly glared at a woman who had just come in. She half-smiled apologetically at him.

"You also live in a blarry tent?"

She struggled with the door and then stood dripping in a pool of wet sawdust. Solly left the counter to add two logs to the furnace. She moved out of the way. Another customer showed indignation at Solly's remarks.

"Fish an' chips. Vinegar? Salt? One an' six. Thank you. Yes, madam?"

"Could you tell me when the bioscope comes out?"

"Am I the blooming manager?"

"Please."

"Half pas' ten, tonight," the Muslim offered helpfully.

"Thank you. Can I stay here till then? It's raining outside."

"I know it's blarrywell raining, but this is not a Salvation Army."

"Please, baas!"

This caught Solly unaware. He had had his shop in that corner of Hanover Street since most could remember and had been called a great many unsavoury things in the years. Solly didn't mind. But this caught him unaware. Please, baas. This felt good. His imagination adjusted a black bow-tie to an evening suit. Please, baas.

"O.K. You stay for a short while. But when 'e rain stops you go!"

She nodded dumbly and tried to make out the blurred name of the cinema opposite, through the misted windows.

"Waiting fer somebody?" Solly asked. No response.

"I ask if yer waiting fer somebody?" The figure continued to stare. "Oh, go to hell," said Solly, turning to another customer.

Through the rain blur Siena stared at nothing in particular. Dim
visions of slippery wet cars. Honking and wheezing in the rain.
Spluttering buses. Heavy, drowsy voices in the Grand Fish and
Chips Palace. Her eyes travelled beyond the street and the water
cascades of Table Mountain, beyond the winter of Cape Town to
the summer of the Boland. Past the green grapelands of Stellen-
bosch and Paarl and the stuffy wheat district of Malmesbury to
the lazy sun and laughter of Teslaarsdal.

Inside the gabled nineteenth-century mission church she had first
met Joseph. The church is quiet and beautiful and the ivy climbs
over it and makes it more beautiful. Huge silver oil lamps suspend-
ed from the roof, polished and shining. It was in the flicker of the
lamps that she had first become aware of him. He was visiting from
Cape Town. She sang that night as she had never sung before.

"Al ging ik ook in een dal der schaduw des doods . . ." Though
I walk through the valley of the shadow of death . . ."der schaduw
des doods." And then he had looked at her. She felt as if everyone
was looking at her.

"Ik zoude geen kwaad vreezen . . ." I will fear no evil. And she
had not feared but loved. Had loved him. Had sung for him. For
the wide eyes, the yellow skin, the high cheekbones. She had sung
for a creator who could create a man like Joseph. "Want gij zijt met
mij; Uw stok en Uw staf, die vertroosten mij."

Those were black-and-white polka-dot nights when the moon did
a golliwog cakewalk across a banjo-strung sky. Nights of sweet
remembrances when he had whispered love to her and told her of
Cape Town. She had giggled coyly at his obscenities. It was
fashionable, she hoped, to giggle coyly at obscenities. He lived in
one of those streets off District Six, it sounded like Horsburg Lane,
and was, he boasted, quite a one with the girls. She heard of Molly
and Miena and Sophia and a sophisticated Charmaine who was
almost a schoolteacher and always spoke English. But he told her

that he had only found love in Teslaarsdal. She wasn't sure whether to believe him. And then he felt her richness, and the moon darted behind a cloud.

The loud screeching of the train to Cape Town. Screeching loud enough to drown the protests of her family. The wrath of her father. The icy stares of Teslaarsdal matrons. Loud and confused screechings to drown her hysteria, her ecstasy. Drowned and confused in the roar of a thousand cars and a hundred thousand lights and a summer of carnival evenings that are Cape Town.

And the agony of the nights when he came home later and later and sometimes not at all. The waning of his passion and whispered names of others. Molly and Miena and Sophia, Charmaine. The helpless knowledge that he was slipping from her. Faster and faster. Gathering momentum.

Not that I'm saying so but I only heard. Why don't you go to bioscope one night and see for yourself? Marian's man is searching for Joseph. Searching for Joseph. Looking for Joseph. Knifing for Joseph. Joseph. Joseph! *Joseph!* Molly! Miena! Sophia! Names! Names! Names! Gossip. One-sided desire. Go to bioscope and see. See what? See why? When? Where?

And after he had been away a week she decided to see. Decided to go through the rain and stand in a sweating fish-and-chips shop owned by a blaspheming and vulgar man. And wait for the cinema to come out.

The rain had stopped sobbing against the plate-glass window. A skin-soaking drizzle now set in. Continuous. Unending. Filming everything with dark depression. A shivering, weeping neon sign flickering convulsively on and off. A tired Solly shooting a quick glance at a cheap alarm clock.

"Half pas' ten, bioscope out soon."

Siena looked more intently through the misty screen. No movement whatsoever in the deserted cinema foyer.

"Time it was bloomingwell out." Solly braced himself for the wave of after-show customers who would invade the Palace.

"Comin' out late tonight, missus."

"Thank you, baas."

Solly rubbed sweat out of his eyes and took in her neat and plain figure. Tired face but good legs. A few late stragglers catching colds in the streets. Wet and squally outside.

"Your man in bioscope?"

She was intent on a khaki-uniformed usher struggling to open the door.

"Man in bioscope, missus?"

The cinema had to come out some time or other. An usher opening the door. Adusting the outside gate. Preparing for the crowds to pour out. To vomit and spill out.

"Man in bioscope?"

No response.

"Oh, go to hell!"

They would be out now. Joseph would be out. She rushed for the door, throwing words of thanks to Solly.

"Close 'e blarry door!"

She never heard him. The drizzle had stopped. An unnatural calm hung over the empty foyer, over the deserted street. She took up her stand on the bottom step. Expectantly. Her heart pounding.

Then they came. Pouring, laughing, pushing, jostling. She stared with fierce intensity, but faces passed too fast. Laughing, roaring, gay. Wide-eyed, yellow-skinned, high-cheekboned. Black, brown, ivory, yellow. Black-eyed, laughing-eyed, bouncing. No Joseph. Palpitating heart that felt like bursting into a thousand pieces. If she should miss him. She found herself searching for the wrong face. Solly's face. Ridiculously searching for hard blue eyes and a sharp white chin in a sea of ebony and brown. Solly's face. Missing half a hundred faces and then again searching for the familiar high cheekbones. Solly. Joseph. Molly. Miena. Charmaine.

The drizzle resumed. Studying overcoats instead of faces. Longing for the pale-blue shirt she had seen in the shop at Solitaire. A bargain for one pound five shillings. She had scraped and scrounged to buy it for him. A week's wages. Collecting her thoughts and continuing the search for Joseph. And then the thinning out of the crowd and the last few stragglers. The ushers shutting the iron gate. They might be shutting Joseph in. Herself out. Only ushers left.

"Please, is Joseph inside?"

"Who's Joseph?"

"Is Joseph still inside?"

"Joseph who?"

They were teasing her. Laughing behind her back. Preventing her from finding him.

"Joseph is inside!" she shouted frenziedly.

"Look, it's raining cats and dogs. Go home."

Go home. To whom. To what? An empty room? An empty bed?

And then she was aware of the crowd on the corner. Maybe he was there. Running and peering into every face. Joseph. The crowd in the drizzle. Two battling figures. Joseph. Figures locked in struggle slithering in the wet gutter. Muck streaking down clothes through which wet bodies were silhouetted. Joseph. A blue shirt. And then she wiped the rain out of her eyes and saw him. Fighting for his life. Desperately kicking in the gutter. Joseph. The blast of a police whistle. A pick-up van screeching to a stop.

"Please, sir, it wasn't him. They all ran away. Please, sir, he's Joseph. He done nothing. He done nothing, my baas. Please, sir, he's my Joseph. Please, baas!"

"Maak dat jy wegkom. Get away. Voetsak!"

"Please, sir, it wasn't him. They ran away!"

Solly's Grand Fish and Chips Palace crowded out. People milling inside. Rain once more squalling and sobbing against the door and windows. Swollen gutters unable to cope with the giddy rush of water. Solly sweating to deal with the after-cinema rush.

Fish an' chips. Vinegar? Salt? One an' six. Thank you. Sorry, no fish yet. Wait five minutes. Chips on'y. Vinegar? Ninepence. Tickey change. Thank you. Sorry, no fish. Five minutes time. Chips? Ninepence. Thank you. Solly paused for breath and stirred the fish.

"What's 'e trouble outside?"

"Real bioscope, Solly."

"No man, outside!"

"I say, real bioscope."

"What were 'e police doing? Sorry, no fish yet, sir. Five minutes time. What were 'e police doin'?"

"A fight in 'e blooming rain."

"Jesus, in 'e rain."

"Ja."

"Who was fighting?"

"Joseph an' somebody."

"Joseph?"

"Ja, fellow in Horsburg Lane."

"Yes, I know Joseph. Always in trouble. Chucked him outta here a'reddy."

"Well, that chap."

"An' who?"

"Dinno."

"Police got them?"

"Got Joseph."

"Why were 'ey fighting? Fish in a minute sir."

"Over a dame."

"Who?"

"You know Marian who works by Patel? Now she. Her boy-friend caught 'em."

"In bioscope?"

"Ja."

Solly chuckled suggestively.

"See that woman an' 'e police."

"What woman?" Solly asked.

"One cryin' to 'e police. They say it's Joseph's girl from 'e country."

"Joseph always got plenty dames from 'e town an' country. F-I-S-H R-E-A-D-Y! Two pieces for you, sir? One an' six. Shilling change. Fish an' chips? One an' six. Thank you. Fish on'y? Vinegar? Salt? Ninepence. Tickey change. Thank you! What you say about 'e woman?"

"They say Joseph's girl was crying to 'e police."

"Oh, he got plenty o' girls."

"This one was living with him."

"Oh, what she look like? Fish, sir?"

"Like 'e country. O.K. Nice legs."

"Hmmmmm," said Solly. "Hey, close 'e damn door. Oh, you again." Siena came in. A momentary silence. Then a buzzing and whispering.

"Oh," said Solly, nodding as someone whispered over the counter to him. "I see. She was waiting here. Musta been waiting for him."

A young girl in jeans giggled.

"Fish an' chips costs one an' six, madam."

"Wasn't it one an' three before?"

"Before the Boer War, madam. Price of fish go up. Potatoes go up an' you expect me to charge one an' three?"

"Why not?"

"Oh, go to hell! Next please!"

"Yes, that's 'e one, Solly."

"Mmmmm. Excuse me, madam," - turning to Siena - "like

some fish an' chips? Free of charge, never min' 'e money."

"Thank you, my baas."

The rain now sobbed wildly as the shop emptied, and Solly counted the cash in his till. Thousands of watery horses charging down the street. Rain drilling into cobbles and pavings. Miniature waterfalls down the sides of buildings. Blurred lights through unending streams. Siena listlessly holding the newspaper parcel of fish and chips.

"You can stay here till it clears up," said Solly.

She looked up tearfully.

Solly grinned showing his yellow teeth. "It's O.K."

A smile flickered across her face for a second.

"It's quite O.K. by me."

She looked down and hesitated for a moment. Then she struggled against the door. It yielded with a crash and the north-wester howled into Solly's Palace.

"Close 'e blarry door!" he said grinning.

"Thank you, my baas," she said as she shivered out into the rain.

The Bench

*This story was influenced by events during the Defiance of Unjust Laws
Campaign during 1952-3.*

"We are part of a complex society further complicated by the fact that the vast majority of the population is denied the very basic privileges of citizenship. Our society condemns a man to an inferior status because he is born black. Our society can only retain its social and economic position at the expense of a large black working-class."

Karlie was concentrating hard while trying to follow the speaker. Something at the back of his mind told him that these were great and true words, whatever they meant. The speaker was a huge black man with a rolling voice. He paused to sip water from a glass. Karlie sweated. The hot October sun beat down mercilessly on the gathering. A burning sky without the slightest vestige of cloud over Table Mountain. The trees on the Grand Parade, drooping and wilted, afforded hardly any shelter. His handkerchief was already soaking where he had placed it around his neck. Karlie looked cautiously at the sea of faces. Black, brown, olive, a few white faces and scattered red fezzes of Muslims. Near a parked car two detectives were taking notes. On the raised platform the rolling voice started again.

"It is up to every one of us to challenge the right of any law which wilfully condemns any person to an inferior position. We must challenge the right of any people to segregate any others on grounds of skin colour. You and your children are denied rights which are yours by virtue of your being South Africans. But you are segregated against politically, socially and economically."

Karlie felt something stirring deep inside him, something he had never experienced before, had never known was there. The man on the platform seemed to be rolling out a new religion which said that he, Karlie, had certain rights, and his children would have certain rights. What sort of rights? Like a white man for instance? To live as well as Oubaas Lategan at Bietjiesfontein? The idea took shape and started developing. A rush of feeling and an insight he had never explored before. To sit at a table in the café at Bietjiesfontein. Nellie and himself ordering steak and eggs and coffee. Sitting downstairs in the local bioscope with the other farmers, and going out at interval to buy drinks at the Panorama. His children attending the Hoërskool and playing rugby and hockey against visiting teams. This was a picture that frightened but at the same time seduced. Now what would Ou Klaas think of that? Ou Klaas who always said that God in his wisdom made the white man white and the coloured man brown and the black man black. And they must know their place. What would Ou Klaas say to such things? Those ideas coming from the platform were far from Ou Klaas and Bietjiesfontein, but in a vague way they made sense.

Karlie knitted his brow while trying to make it all out. There were many others on the platform, black and white and brown. And they behaved as if there were no difference in colour. What would Ou Klaas say when he told him about it? Oubaas Lategan? A white woman in a blue dress offering a cigarette to the previous speaker who was a black man? He had been introduced as Mr Nxeli, a trade-union leader who had often been in jail. A white woman offering him a cigarette. Karlie also felt like smoking and took out a crumpled packet of Cavalla.

Imagine if Ou Klaas offered Annetjie Lategan a suck at his pipe. What would her father say? Oubaas Lategan would most probably get his gun and shoot him on the spot. The idea was so ludicrous that Karlie burst out laughing. One or two people looked round inquiringly. In a fit of embarrassment he converted the laugh into a cough and lit the mangled cigarette. But his mind refused to give up the picture. And Annetjie was nowhere near as pretty and had no such blue, shop-bought dress. When the lady on the platform moved, her dress was tight around her. He saw that when she offered Mr Nxeli a cigarette.

If all the things the speaker said were true, it meant that he, Karlie, was as good as any other man. His mouth played with the

words, "even a white man," but he quickly dispelled this notion.
But the speaker seemed to be emphasising just that. And why
should he not accept those ideas? He remembered being shown
a picture torn out of a newspaper of those people who defied laws
which they said were unjust. He had asked Ou Klaas about it but
the old man had merely shrugged his shoulders. The people in
the newspaper were smiling as they went to prison. These things
were confusing and strange.

The speaker with the rolling voice continued and Karlie listened
intently. He seemed so sure and confident of himself as the words
flowed out. Karlie felt sure that he was even greater than Oubaas
Lategan or even the dominee of the whites-only church in Bietjiesfontein. The lady in the blue dress spoke next. The one who had
given Mr Nxeli a cigarette. She said that one must challenge all
discriminatory laws. It was one's duty to do so. All laws which said
that one person was inferior to another. "Sit anywhere you wish,
whether in a train or a restaurant. Let them arrest you if they dare."
The white detectives were very busy taking notes. Why should she
be telling them this? She could go to the best bioscopes, swim off
the best beaches, live in the best areas. What made a white woman
who could have everything say such words? And she was far more
beautiful than Annetjie Lategan and had hair that gleamed with
gold in the sun.

He had been worried before he left Bietjiesfontein that things
would be different in Cape Town. He had seen the skollies in
Hanover Street but they no longer held any terror for him, although
he had been frightened at first. He now lived off Caledon Street
near Star Bioscope. He had very few friends, one in Athlone whom
he was going to visit when he saw the meeting on the Grand Parade.
District Six proved a bit of a let-down, but no one, not even Ou
Klaas, had warned him about the things he was now hearing. This

was new. This set the mind racing. The lady emphasised that they should challenge these laws and suffer the consequences. Yes, he must challenge. The resolve started shaping in his mind but still seemed far too daring, far too ridiculous. But as the lady continued, a determination started creeping over the vagueness. Yes, he must challenge. He, Karlie, would challenge and suffer the consequences. He would astound Oubaas Lategan and Ou Klaas and Annetjie and Nellie when they saw his picture in the newspaper. And he would smile. He would even astound the lady in the blue dress. With the fervency of a new convert he determined that he was going to challenge, even if it meant prison. He would smile like those people in the newspaper.

The meeting passed a resolution, then sang 'Nkosi Sikelel' iAfrika' and they all raised their hands with the thumbs pointing up and shouted "Afrika!" And then the crowd dispersed. Karlie threaded his way through the mass to get to the station. His friend would be waiting for him in Athlone. The words of all the speakers still milled in his head. Confusing somehow but at the same time quite clear. He must challenge. This could never have happened at Bietjiesfontein, or could it? The sudden screech of a car as brakes were applied. Karlie jumped out of the way just in time. A head was angrily thrust through the window.

"Look where you're going, you bloody baboon!"

Karlie stared dazed, momentarily too stunned to speak. Surely the driver could not have seen the white woman offering Mr Nxeli a cigarette? She would never have shouted at him like that and called him a baboon. She had said one must challenge. These things were all so confusing. Maybe best to catch a train and get to his friend in Athlone and tell him all about it. He had to speak to someone.

He saw the station through the eyes of a fresh convert. A mass of human beings, mostly white but with some blacks and a few browns like himself. Here they pushed and jostled but there seemed

a cocoon around each person. Each one in his own world. Each
moving in a narrow pattern of his own manufacture. But one must
challenge these things the woman had said. And the man with the
rolling voice. Each in his own way. But how did one challenge?
What did one challenge?

Then it dawned on him. Here was his chance. The bench. The
railway bench with the legend WHITES ONLY neatly painted on it
in white.

For a moment it symbolised all the misery of South African
society. Here was his challenge to his rights as a man. Here it stood.
A perfectly ordinary wooden bench like the hundreds of thousands
of others all over South Africa. Benches on dusty stations in the
Karoo; under ferns and subtropical foliage in Natal; benches all
over the country each with its legend. His challenge. That bench
now had concentrated in it all the evils of a system he could not
understand. It was the obstacle between himself and his manhood.
If he sat on it, he was a man. If he was afraid, he denied himself
membership as a human in human society. He almost had visions
of righting the system if only he sat on that bench. Here was his
chance. He, Karlie, would challenge.

He seemed perfectly calm as he sat down, but his heart was
thumping wildly. Two conflicting ideas now seeped through him.
The one said, 'You have no right to sit on the bench.' The other
questioned, 'Why have you no right to sit on the bench?' The first
spoke of the past, of the life on the farm, of the servile figure of
his father and Ou Klaas, his father's father who had said, 'God
in his wisdom made the white man white and the black man black.'
The other voice had promise of the future in it and said, 'Karlie,
you are a man. You have dared what your father would not have
dared. And his father. You will die like a man.'

Karlie took out a Cavalla from the crumpled packet and smoked.
But nobody seemed to notice him sitting there. This was also a

let-down. The world still pursued its natural way. People still lived, breathed and laughed. No voice shouted triumphantly, 'Karlie, you have conquered!' He was a perfectly ordinary human being sitting on a bench on a crowded station, smoking a cigarette. Or was this his victory? Being an ordinary human being sitting on a bench?

A well-dressed white lady walked down the platform. Would she sit on the bench? And the gnawing voice, 'You should stand up and let the white woman sit. This bench is not for you.' Karlie's eyes narrowed as he pulled more fiercely at his cigarette. She swept past with scarcely a glance at him. Was she afraid of challenging his rights to be a human being? Or couldn't she care less?

Karlie now realised that he was completely exhausted. He was used to physical work but this was different. He was mentally and emotionally drained. A third conflicting thought now crept in, a compensatory one which said, 'You do not sit on the bench to challenge. You sit here because you are tired, therefore you are sitting here.' He would not move because he was tired. He wanted to rest. Or was it because he wanted to challenge?

People were now pouring from the Athlone train that had pulled in at the platform. There were so many pushing and jostling one another that nobody seemed to have time to notice him. When the train pulled out it would pass Athlone. It would be the easiest thing in the world to step into it and ride away from all this. He could rest because he was tired. Away from challenges, and benches one was not allowed to sit on. And meetings on the Grand Parade. And a white lady offering Mr Nxeli a cigarette. But that would be giving in, suffering a personal defeat, refusing to challenge. In fact it would be admitting that he was not a human being . . .

He sat on smoking another cigarette and allowing his mind to wander. Far away from the station and the bench. Bietjiesfontein and that talk he had had with his grandfather when he had told Ou Klaas what he had on his mind. The glittering lights of Cape

Town and better jobs and more money so that he could send some home. Ou Klaas had looked up quizzically while sucking at his pipe. Ou Klaas was wise and had lived long. He always insisted that one must learn through travelling. He had lived in Cape Town as a young man and would spit and laugh slyly when he told of the girls in District Six. Beautiful, olive-skinned and doe-eyed. Ou Klaas knew everything. He also said that God in his wisdom made the white man white and the black man black. And each must keep his place.

"You are sitting on the wrong seat." Karlie did not notice the person speaking. Ou Klaas had a trick of spitting on the ground and pulling his mouth slyly when he made a strong point, especially about the women he had had.

"This is the wrong seat."

Karlie whipped back to reality. He was going to get up instinctively when he realised who he was and why was sitting there. He suddenly felt very tired and looked up slowly. A thin, gangling, pimple-faced white youth lugging an enormous suitcase.

"I'm sorry but you on the wrong seat. This is for whites only."

Karlie stared at him saying nothing.

"Are you deaf? You are sitting on the wrong bench. This is not for you people. It is for white people only."

Slowly and deliberately Karlie puffed at his cigarette and examined it exaggeratedly. This was the test, or the contest? The white youth was sizing him up.

"If you don't move now you can get into serious trouble."

Karlie maintained his obstinate silence. The youth was obviously not going to take the law into his own hands. For Karlie to speak now would be to break the spell, the supremacy he felt he was gaining.

"Well, you asking for it. I will have to report you."

Karlie realised that the youth was brazening it out, afraid to take action himself. He went off leaving his suitcase on the bench next to Karlie. He, Karlie, had won the first round of the bench dispute.

He took out another cigarette. Irresolution had now turned to determination. Under no circumstances was he going to give up his bench. They could do what they wanted. He stared hostilely at the suitcase.

"Come on, you're sitting on the wrong bench. There are seats further down for you people." The policeman towered over him. Karlie could see thin red hairs on his neck. The white youth stood behind the officer. Karlie said nothing.

"I'm ordering you to move for the last time."

Karlie remained seated.

"All right. Then I want your name and address and you will come with me." Karlie maintained the obstinate silence. This took the policeman unawares. The crowd started growing and one joker shouted "Afrika!" and then disappeared among the spectators.

"I will have to place you under arrest. Come on, get up."

Karlie remained seated. The policeman grabbed him by the shoulders, assisted by the white youth. Karlie turned to resist, to cling to the bench, to his bench. He hit out wildly and then felt a dull pain as a fist rammed into his stomach. He rolled onto the ground grazing his face against the rough tarmac. Then his arms were twisted behind him and handcuffs bit into his wrists. Suddenly he relaxed and struggled to his feet. It was senseless fighting any longer. Now it was his turn to smile. He had challenged and felt he had won. If not a victory over them, then one over himself. Who cared about the consequences? The white youth was dusting his trousers.

"Come on," said the policeman forcing Karlie through the crowd.

"Certainly," said Karlie for the first time, and stared at the crowd with the arrogance of one who had dared to sit on a WHITES ONLY bench.

Resurrection

And still they sang. One by one the voices joined in and the volume rose. Tremulously at first, thin and cloying and then swelling till it filled the tiny dining-room, pulsated into the two bedrooms stacked high with hats and overcoats, and spent itself in the kitchen where housewives were fussing over wreaths.

Jesu, lover of my soul, Let me to Thy bosom fly. A blubbery woman in the corner nearest the cheap, pine chest of drawers, dabbed her eyes with pink tissues. Above her head hung a cheap reproduction of an English cottage smothered with creepers and flowers and, embossed beneath, What is a Home without a Mother? The woman heaved convulsively as she refused to be placated. Her tears proved infectious and other lips quivered and tissues and handkerchiefs were hurriedly sought.

A small boy in a navy-blue suit shared a stiff *Ancient and Modern* with his mother. His voice was wispy and completely dominated by the quivering soprano next to him. All sang except Mavis. She sat silent, glassy-eyed, staring down at her rough though delicately carved brown hand. Her eyes were red but tearless with a slightly contemptuous sneer around the closed, cruel mouth. Mavis sat silently staring at her hand, half-noticing that the left thumbnail was scarred and broken at the edge. She did not raise her eyes to look at the coffin or at the hymnbook closed and neglected in her lap. Her mouth was tight-shut, determined not to open, not to say a word. She sat tensely staring at the broken nail. The room did not exist nor the boy in the navy-blue suit nor the fat lady nor any of the people. Although they sang Mavis seemed not to hear.

Other refuge have I none, Hangs my helpless soul on Thee. The fat woman had recovered sufficiently to attempt a tremulous contralto. The boy tried to follow the line without using his finger. Mavis vaguely recognised Rosie, as her sister fussily hurried in with a tray of fresh flowers, passed a brief word with an overdressed woman nearest the door and busily hurried out again. Mavis sensed things happening but saw without seeing and felt without feeling. Nothing seemed to register but she could feel the Old-Woman's presence, could feel the room becoming her dead mother, becoming full of Ma, crowded with Ma, swirling with Ma. Ma of the swollen hands and frightened eyes who had asked almost petulantly, "Mavis, why do they treat me so? Please, Mavis, why do they treat me so?"

Mavis knew the answer and felt the anger welling up inside her till her mouth felt hot and raw. And she spoke in a tense monotone, "Because you're black. You're black, Ma, but you gave birth to white children. It's all your fault. You gave birth to white children, Ma."

Mavis felt dimly aware that the room was overcrowded, overbearingly overcrowded, hot, stuffy, crammed to overflowing. With Ma squeezed in and occupying a tiny place in the centre. Pride of place in a coffin of pine-wood bearing the economical legend, Maria Wilhelmina Loupser, R.I.P. Rest in Peace. With people crowding around and sharing seats and cramming the doorway. To see Ma who had been Maria Loupser. Maria Wilhelmina Loupser. Mavis looked up quickly to see if the plaque was still on the coffin, then automatically shifted her gaze to the broken nail. No-one noticed her and the singing continued uninterruptedly.

Other refuge have I none, Hangs my helpless soul on Thee. Flowers. The hot, oppressive smell of flowers. Flowers, death and the people singing. The smell of death in the flowers. A florid, red-faced man in the doorway singing so that the veins stood out purple against the temples. People bustling in and out, struggling through the doorway. Coming to have a look at Ma, a last look. To put a flower in the coffin, then open hymnbooks and sing for poor, deceived Ma of the twisted hands and tragic eyes. Ma who had given birth to white children and Mavis. Now they raised their voices and sang. All except Mavis.

It had been only a month before when Mavis had looked into those bewildered eyes.

"Mavis, why do they treat me so?"

And Mavis had suddenly become angry so that her saliva burned in her mouth.

"Please, Mavis, tell me why do they treat me so?"

And then she had driven the words into the Old-Woman. "Because you are old and ugly and black, and your children want you out of the way."

What she really wanted to say was, "They want me out of the way too. They treat me like that also, because you made me, you made me black like you. I am also your child. I also belong to you. They want me also to stay in the kitchen and use the back door like you. We must not be seen, Ma. Their friends must not see us. Dadda's people must not see us because we embarrass them. They hate us, ma. They hate us both because they see themselves in us." But she had not said so and had only stared cruelly into the eyes of the Old-Woman.

"You see, you're no longer useful to scrub and wash and cook. You're a nuisance, a bloody nuisance. You might come out of your kitchen and shock the white scum they bring here. You're a bloody black nuisance, Ma."

The Old-Woman could not understand and looked helplessly at Mavis, shutting her eyes with her swollen hands.

"But I don't want to go into the dining-room. It's true, Mavis, I don't want to go into the dining-room." And as she spoke the tears squeezed through her fingers and ran over her thick knuckles. She whimpered like a child.

"It's my dining-room, Mavis, it's true. I also worked for it. It's my dining room."

And Mavis felt a dark and hideous pleasure overwhelming her so that she shouted at the Old-Woman. "Don't you understand that

you are black and your bloody children are white! Jim and Rosie
and Sonny are white! And you made me like you. You made me
black!"

Then Mavis broke down exhausted at her self-revelation and cried
with the Old-Woman.

"Ma, why did you make me black?"

And then only had a vague understanding strayed into those
milky eyes, and Ma had taken her youngest into her arms and
rocked and soothed her, crooning to her in a cracked, broken voice
the songs she had sung years before she had come to Cape Town.
Slaap, my kindjie, slaap sag, Onder engele vannag. And the voice
of the Old-Woman had become stronger and more perceptive and
her dull eyes saw her childhood and the stream running through
Wolfgat and the solidly built church, and the moon rising rich and
yellow in the direction of Solitaire.

And Ma had vaguely understood and rocked Mavis in her arms
as in years before. And now she was back in the dining-room as
shadows crept across the wall. Fast falls the eventide. Creeping
across the wall ever greyer. The darkness deepens. Filtering across
the drawn blind. Rosie, tight-lipped and officious. Sonny. Jim who
had left his fair-skinned wife at home. Pointedly ignoring Mavis.
Speaking in hushed tones to a florid man in the doorway. Mavis,
a small inconspicuous brown figure in the corner. The only other
brown face in the crowded room besides Ma. And even the Old-
Woman was paler in death.

Ma's friends in the kitchen. A huddled, frightened group sitting
out of the way of the wreath-makers. Warming themselves at the
stove.

"Mavis, why do they tell my friends not to visit me?"

And Mavis had shrugged her shoulders indifferently.

"Please, Mavis, why do they tell my friends not to visit me?"

And Mavis had turned on her, appalled at her naïveté.

"Do you want Soufie to sit in the dining-room? Or Ou-Kaar? Or Eva or Leuntjie? Do you want Sonny's wife to have tea with them? Or the white dirt Rosie brings home? Do you want to shame your children? Humiliate them? Show their friends who their mother really is?"

And the Old-Woman had blubbered, "I only want my friends to visit me. They can sit with me in the kitchen."

And Mavis had sighed helplessly at the simplicity of the doddering Old-Woman and had felt like saying, "And what of my friends? Must they also sit in the kitchen?" And tears had shot into the milky eyes and the Old-Woman had looked even older. "Mavis, I want my friends to visit me, even if they sit in the kitchen. Please, Mavis, they're all I got left."

And now they sat in the kitchen, a cowed, timid group speaking the raw, guttural Afrikaans of the Caledon district. They spoke of Ma and their childhood together. Ou-Kaar and Leuntjie and Eva and Ma. Of the Caledon district cut off from surging Cape Town. Where the Moravian church stood solidly and sweet water ran past Wolfgat and past Karwyderskraal and lost itself near Grootkop. And the moon rose rich and yellow from the hills behind Solitaire. And now they sat frightened and huddled around the stove speaking of Ma. Tant Soufie in a new kopdoek and Ou-Kaar conspicuous in yellow velskoene sizes too big, and Leuntjie and Eva.

And in the dining-room sat Dadda's relations and friends singing. Dadda's relations and friends who had ignored Ma while she had lived. Dadda's fair friends and relations. And a Mavis who scratched meaninglessly at her broken thumbnail she did not see.

And now the singing rose in volume as still more people filed in. When other helpers fail and comfort flee, Help of the helpless, O abide with me. Mavis could have helped Ma, could have given her the understanding she needed, could have protected her and stopped the petty tyranny. But she had never tried to reason with

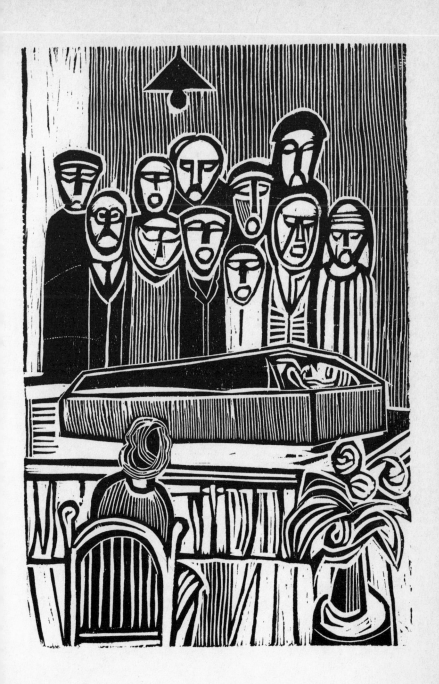

them, explained to them that the Old-Woman was dying. Her own
hurt ate into her, gnawed at her. So she preferred to play a shadow,
seen but never heard. A vague entity, part of the furniture. If only
they knew of the feelings bottled up inside her. She was afraid that
if they did they might say, "Why don't you both clear out and leave
us in peace, you bloody black bastards?" She could then have
cleared out, should then have cleared out, sought a room in
Woodstock or Salt River and forgotten her frustrations. But there
was Ma. There was always the Old-Woman. Mavis never spoke to
them, only to Ma.

"You sent them to a white school. You were proud of your brats
and hated me, didn't you, Ma?"

And the mother had stared at her with ox-like dumbness.

"You encouraged them to bring their friends to the house, to your
house, and stayed in the kitchen yourself and told me to stay there
too. You hated me, Ma, hated me, because I was yourself. There's
no-one to blame but you. You caused all this. You encouraged all
this."

And she had tormented the Old-Woman, who could not retaliate,
who could not understand. Now she sat tortured with memories
as they sang hymns for Ma. I need Thy presence every passing
hour, sang Dadda's eldest brother, who sat with eyes tightly shut
near the head of the coffin. He had bitterly resented Dadda's mar-
riage to a Bushman from God-knows-where in the country. A
bloody disgrace. A Loupser married to a coloured. He had refused
to greet Ma socially while she lived, and attended the funeral only
because his late brother's wife had died. It was the decent thing
to do. This was the second time he had been in the dining-room.
The first was at Dadda's funeral. And now this. A coloured girl,
his niece he believed, sitting completely out of place and saying
nothing. Most annoying and embarrassing.

The boy in the navy-blue suit continued to sing weakly. His

mother had not quite recovered from the shock that that nice Mr
Loupser who always used to visit them in Observatory, was married to a coloured woman. All sang except Mavis.

"I am going to die, Mavis," the milky eyes had told her a week
before. "I think I am going to die."

"Ask your white brats to bury you. You slaved enough for them."

"They are my children but they do not treat me right."

"Do you know why? Because they are ashamed of you. Afraid
of you. Afraid the world might find out about you."

"But I did my best for them."

"You did more than your best, you encouraged them. But you
were ashamed of me, weren't you? So now we share a room at the
back where we can't be seen. And you are going to die and your
children will thank God that you're out of the way."

"I am your mother, my girl, I raised you."

"Yes, you raised me and taught me my place. You took me to the
Mission with you because you felt we were too black to go to St
John's. Let them see Pastor Josephs for a change. Let them enter
our Mission and see our God."

And Ma had not understood and said whiningly, "Please, Mavis,
let Pastor Josephs bury me."

So now the priest from Dadda's church stood at the head of her
coffin, sharp and thin, clutching his cassock with the left hand
while his right held an open prayerbook.

I said I will take heed to my ways: that I offend not in my tongue.
I will keep my mouth as it were with a bridle while the ungodly
is in my sight.

Mavis felt the full irony of the words.

I held my tongue and spake nothing. I kept silent, yea even from
good words, but it was pain and grief to me.

The fat lady stroked her son's head and sniffed loudly.

My heart was hot within me, and while I was thus musing the

fire kindled, and at the last I spake with my tongue.

Mavis now stared entranced at her broken fingernail. The words seared and burnt through her.

It was true. Rosie had consulted her about going to the Mission and asking Pastor Josephs but Mavis had turned on her heel without a word and walked out into the street and walked and walked. Through the cobbled streets of older Cape Town, up beyond the Mosque in the Malay Quarter on the slopes of Signal Hill. Thinking of the dead woman. A mother dying in a backroom. Walking the streets, the Old-Woman with her, followed by the Old-Woman's eyes. Let them go to the Mission and see our God. Meet Pastor Josephs. But they had gone to Dadda's priest, who now prayed at the coffin of a woman he had never seen before.

I heard a voice from heaven, Saying unto me, Write. From henceforth blessed are the dead which die in the Lord: Even so saith the Spirit; for they rest from their labours.

Lord, take Thy servant, Maria Wilhelmina Loupser into Thy eternal care. Grant her Thy eternal peace and understanding. Thou art our refuge and our rock. Look kindly upon her children gathered here who even in their hour of trial and suffering look up to Thee for solace. Send Thy eternal blessing upon them, for they have heeded Thy commandment which is to honour thy father and thy mother that thy days may be long.

Mavis felt hot, strangely, unbearably hot. The room was filled with her mother's presence, her mother's eyes, body. Flowing into her, filling every pore, becoming one with her. She knew she had to control herself or she would scream out blasphemies, invectives, the truth. Slowly she stood up and, without looking at the coffin or anyone around her, left the room.

No Room at Solitaire

Now Fanie van der Merwe had every right to be annoyed. Here he stood, owner of the only hotel in Solitaire, wiping glasses in an empty bar on Christmas Eve. Christmas Eve of all times. The owner of the only canteen before Donkergat, and facing empty tables and chairs. Well, not quite empty, because old Dawie Volkwyn sat sullen and morose at the counter. Fanie couldn't remember when Dawie had not sat on the very same stool opposite the kitchen door. To have the only canteen for goodness-knows-how-many-miles-around empty on Christmas Eve.

It was obviously done for spite. Oom Sarel Louw always did things for spite. The most spiteful and the richest farmer in the district. Take the time when his daughter, Marietjie, went out with Dawie.

Oom Sarel's argument with Fanie had begun over politics. Oom Sarel had sat at the counter, the way he always sat, holding forth on every subject. God's gift to South African politics, Fanie had mumbled under his breath. Fanie had kept calm until Oom Sarel had said that blacks could not be educated beyond Standard Six. Yes, he knew that some of them were doctors and such things but that was a plot. Fanie had been annoyed, very annoyed, and had quoted the case of Witbooi's cousin. Now Witbooi's cousin had reached Standard Eight at a school in Cape Town. Oom Sarel had insisted that it was unheard of, and if it were so it was deliberately done by the English or progressives or something like that. Fanie had added that Witbooi's cousin could read and write in Afrikaans even better than some of the white bywoners. Oom Sarel had become very red about the neck and had said he would not drink in a bar owned by a man who had sold his people to the communists. Then he had walked out. Now Fanie knew that he, Fanie, was argumentative and that many had walked out before. But Oom Sarel was different. He owned 'Bo-Plaas', the richest wheat farm in the district, and had already been to Johannesburg twice and sometimes visited Hermanus for his holidays.

So it was obviously done for spite. Otherwise why should Oom Sarel have a Christmas Eve braaivleis and invite everyone in Solitaire except Fanie van der Merwe and, well, and Dawie Volkwyn? The free boerewors and brandy were given to lure away all his customers. Louw Viljoen and Daantjie Pretorius and Jan Mostert and them. Fanie would have loved to be there. He could easily have closed the bar and given Witbooi the evening off. But then he had been pointedly ignored.

So now he half-heartedly wiped glasses on Christmas Eve and surveyed the deserted canteen. Only Dawie. But then no one ever invited Dawie anywhere. Yet, in spite of his drinking and bad reputation with women, Dawie Volkwyn knew life. And when he had had sufficient brandy, he would belch, lean back comfortably, narrow his eyes, and hold forth on religion, politics, the English, the blacks, why the world was going to the dogs, and Marietjie Louw. He was certain that Marietjie was a little more than interested in him but Oom Sarel thought Dawie too old at fifty. Marietjie herself must be well over forty, and there was no prospect of a husband in sight.

"Ja, Dawie," said Fanie, sitting down opposite him, "so goes the world."

Dawie made no reply, so Fanie opened a bottle of brandy and filled two glasses. They drank in silence, each occupied with his own thoughts.

Fanie filled again. "It is hard when there is no business."

Another long silence while they sipped their brandy. After the third glass Dawie replied.

"I hear Oom Sarel slaughtered two oxen."

"Ja."

"And three lambs, and fowls and geese."

"Ja."

"And Oom Sarel bought all the wine and brandy from Cohen in Donkergat."

"Ja," repeated Fanie fatalistically. He began to have serious doubts about the ability of Witbooi's cousin to read and write in Afrikaans. He would have to ask his kitchen boy. Witbooi's cousin was beginning to mess up his business.

"I never would have thought my bar would be empty on Christmas Eve."

"So goes the world."

"To buy all his spirits from a Jew in Donkergat."

Fanie poured Dawie another drink.

"Well, here's to Christmas. Veels geluk."

"Veels geluk."

"A long time ago in Bethlehem."

"Ja," said Dawie looking far back in time, far beyond his fifty years. "It was a long time ago."

"But He will return."

"It says so in the Book."

"Ja."

"In Revelation."

"He will come in all His glory."

"And the trumpets shall sound."

"But I've been thinking, Fanie."

"Ja?"

"When He first came they didn't know Him."

"So?"

"It stands so in the Book."

"I know that."

"How will we know Him when He comes again?"

"You are speaking dangerous things."

"What if He is not a white man?"

"He is a white man!"

"I know," Dawie said weakly, thinking of the remaining brandy.

They slipped back into silence and Fanie automatically refilled the glasses.

"How will we recognise Him?"

"There will be signs, Dawie."

"Like what?"

"It stands so in the Book."

Fanie had hoped that Louw Viljoen, Jan Mostert and Daantjie Pretorius would still come in for a quick one, even if Oom Sarel's wine was free. So he bought it from a Jew in Donkergat and not one of his own people. Sheer spite.

"Fanie, I'm not a religious man."

"I know, Dawie."

"I'm not a church-going man."

"I know."

"But I'm a questioning man."

"Ja."

"And the question I want to ask is how will we know Him when He comes again?"

"It stands so in the Book."

"What does it say?"

"You must read it in the Book."

"I'm not a reading man."

"Ja." Fanie felt that the conversation was leading nowhere, and decided to revert to the subject of Witbooi's cousin.

"Do you believe they can read?"

"Who?"

"The black people."

"I suppose so, Fanie."

"If they went to school in Cape Town?"

"Maybe, Fanie."

"That's what I told Oom Sarel."

"And so?"

"Called me a kafferboetie."

"Wragtig."

"And a communist."

"That is bad."

"So I told him about Witbooi's cousin."

"Ja?"

"You know him?"

"No."

"He passed Standard Eight."

"That can be."

"Then Oom Sarel walked out on me."

Both men moodily sipped at their glasses. Dawie wondered whether Marietjie Louw was also at 'Bo-Plaas'. She must be since it was owned by her father. Was she thinking of him? Fanie hoped that Louw Viljoen and Daantjie Pretorius would drop in after the braaivleis. If only to tell him how it went. He liked Louw.

"Baas!"

"Ja, Witbooi?"

"There's a man with a woman outside who wants to see the baas."

"Tell them to come right in."

"Baas, they are from my people."

"Then tell them to go to hell." He turned to Dawie. "They are becoming more and more cheeky."

"That is true."

"A lazy bunch of good-for-nothings."

"I agree with you."

"But that doesn't mean some can't read and write."

"True."

"In English and Afrikaans."

"That is so."

"Take Witbooi's cousin."

"Ja, Witbooi's cousin."

The kitchen hand reappeared, greatly agitated.

"Baas, the man say it is serious."

"Chase them away."

"I tried to, baas."

"Tell them I'll come with my shotgun."

"It's no use, baas."

"Get rid of them."

"I try again, baas."

Fanie removed a fresh bottle of brandy from the shelf and twisted off the cap with a flourish. He squinted expertly at the bottle and filled the two glasses, feeling much better, even jovial.

"Now take Witbooi's cousin."

"Ja."

"Now there's a clever skepsel."

"Must be."

"He works in an office in Cape Town."

"Ja?"

"Writes letters for the boss."

"Wragtig!"

"And at the end of the month he sends out accounts."

"Some of those people can do it."

"But Oom Sarel can't understand."

"Oom Sarel is a difficult man," said Dawie with conviction. Witbooi tapped Fanie lightly on the sleeve.

"Please, baas, come and see."

"What?"

"The man and the woman at the back-door."

"Didn't you chase them away?"

"I can't, baas."

"Verdomp! Bring my shotgun!"

"Ja, baas."

"Kom, Dawie, let's get rid of them."

Dawie was reluctant to shift from the half-full bottle of brandy, but had to be careful not to annoy Fanie. He climbed unsteadily to his feet and swayed behind the hotel-keeper through the canteen and kitchen.

In the doorway stood a bearded man of indefinite age. A black woman was groaning next to him.

"Ja?" asked Fanie.

"My wife, she is sick."

"So what is wrong with her?"

"She is sick, baas."

"But what is the matter?"

"She is going to have a child."

"I am not a verdomde midwife."

"I look for a doctor, baas."

"Ja?"

"There's no one in the dorp."

"So what can I do about it?"

"They all at 'Bo-Plaas'. "

"So?"

"I need help, baas, my wife is sick."

An ugly gleam crept into Fanie's eyes. "Why don't you go to 'Bo-Plaas'?"

"She is sick, baas."

"Come on, get away. The doctor is at 'Bo-Plaas'. "

"Please, baas."

"Voetsek!" Fanie turned on his heels, followed by Dawie. They settled down again to their drinks.

"As if I'm a verdomde midwife."

"They are getting more cheeky."

"To come to me of all people."

"Wragtig."

"I run an hotel, I don't deliver babies."

"That's the worst of those people."

The gleam crept back into Fanie's eyes. "I hope they go to 'Bo-Plaas'."

"Ja?"

"That would put Oom Sarel in his place."

"That would."

"And the woman must give birth right there in the middle of the boerewors."

"That would be too funny."

"Please, baas."

Fanie turned around, annoyed at Witbooi.

"They're still here, baas."

"Huh?"

"They won't go away."

"Chase them."

"They want a place to rest."

"There's no room."

"In one of the barns, baas."

"There's no place."

"The woman is very sick."

Fanie downed his brandy at one gulp and drank two more in quick succession. "There's no room!" he repeated, then stared amazed at Dawie, who had begun to laugh hysterically in a high-pitched, drunken giggle.

"And what do you find so funny?"

"There's no room," Dawie repeated, "no room at the inn."

"And so?"

"Can't you see, man?"

"No."

"It's Christmas Eve."

"Allewêreld!"

"Ja! ja!" Fanie burst out in a guffaw, but there was a false ring. He choked, spluttered and then burst out into a fit of coughing. He recovered and laughed till the tears streamed down his cheeks. Dawie laughed dutifully.

"No room at the inn."

"Ja, that is very funny."

Fanie was suddenly silent. Dawie stifled a half-hearted attempt to laugh.

"Come, let's go and see," Fanie said suddenly.

"All right."

"Bring the brandy along."

"And the glasses."

They got up unsteadily and walked to the back-door. Fanie looked ash-grey under his leathery skin. There was no one there.

"Witbooi!"

No reply.

"Witbooi!"

The servant appeared suddenly as if from nowhere.

"Baas?"

"Where's the man?"

"I don't know, baas."

"You're lying."

"It's true, baas."

"Where are they?"

"The woman is very sick."

"So where did they go?"

"I gave them shelter, baas. The woman is very sick."

"Yes, but where?"

"With the donkeys and the mules, baas."

"Hemelsnaam!"

"Allewêreld!"

Fanie and Dawie slowly looked at each other and then, at the same time, timidly looked towards the sky to see whether there was a bright star.

Drive-in

It wasn't really a meeting, rather an informal get-together, a social occasion of would-be writers and weekend poets who wished to have regular discussions. Dambisa was starting to worry about getting home. Two buses and a train to catch. Maybe only one bus and a train if he could walk fast enough to the station from Oranjezicht. Then the train to Claremont and, with luck, the last bus to Guguletu. Oranjezicht was a lifetime of experience away from Guguletu. Oranjezicht was peaceful and tranquil under the dark, brooding mass of Table Mountain. Guguletu was bare with matchbox on matchbox stretching as far as the eye could see with only crudely scrawled numbers to distinguish one house from another. N.Y.1 or N.Y.13. N.Y. . . . Native Yard as he used to call it. A bus to the station, a train to Claremont and with luck the bus to Guguletu. Or else the long walk along lonely Lansdowne Road past dark dangerous deserts like Hanover Park.

The discussion had taken place at Mervyn's flat, where he had been once before. Cheap wine, potato crisps and lots of smoke. Crude African mats on the floor with Skotnes prints on the wall. Rows and rows of untidy paperbacks. The discussion had continued interminably. The establishment of a multiracial writers' group, or was it non-racial? This had caused much argument and drinking. Mr Dambisa, you are our contact. There must be many poets and writers in Guguletu and Langa. Do you think they will come if we invite them to our readings? You must tell us. Our problem is lack of communication. After all you've met Sipho Sepamla and we believe Professor Mphahlele has addressed you people once. We all find the subject of negritude fascinating. Senghor quite sends me.

At last it seemed to be over, or at least was petering out. His head was throbbing from the white wine he had been forced to consume, and from inhaling all that cigarette smoke. If only he could be alone for a while to collect his thoughts. It would be all right in the buses and the train. At least passengers in third class did not ask inane questions. They either accosted you or left you alone. He would be able to withdraw into himself. Unless he met someone he knew, which was highly unlikely.

"Care for a lift?" It was Jenny. Godammit, couldn't that woman ever leave him alone?

"It's quite all right, thanks. I'll take a bus to town."

"Where do you have to get to?"

"Guguletu. It's far too far for you to go."

"But surely I can drop you somewhere along the way?"

"I'll be quite all right. Thanks for the offer."

He had first met her at another of those discussions-cum-parties at Mervyn's. Mervyn was always finding some pretext for getting people together. He did not want to go but Mervyn had insisted. We want views from the other side. He liked Mervyn and did not want to give offence, so went, vowing never to go again. And there he had met Jenny for the first time. Jenny was ostentatiously progressive and liberal. She loved blacks; their lives were so full and not empty like the unthinking white rugby player or the girls who sold records in the CNA. Take the Soweto poets for instance. Why was Gwala so bitter? Angry but his anger was understandable. She thought *Umabatha* an improvement on *Macbeth*. It brings it all so near; makes it all so relevant. Dambisa tried to close his ears to her prattle that went on and on. A ribbon of sound. He sensed that under all the enthusiasm was a lonely person who, in spite of all the babbling, was sensitive. Or was she? She phoned him after she had read two of his poems in *Staffrider* and said that she was convinced that he was destined to become a famous black writer. She meant this seriously. He had avoided her until this second time at Mervyn's.

"But it will really be no problem. I'm sure I can drop you somewhere along the way," she persisted.

He felt uncomfortable when he resisted such considerateness. He felt even more uncomfortable when he accepted it. Why must she be so kind in such a persistent way? It annoyed him, not because she was white but because she tried so hard to be accommodating. If only she would stop gushing. He was tired. The evening was a non-event as far as he was concerned. He should never have come. The room full of smoke and their constantly referring to him as the only black present. The way they hung on his every word, listening intently as if he were the oracle for every oppressed black in South Africa. When he said he was not up to their expectations they made allowances for that also.

"I'm sorry but I must get home. I've had a heavy day."

"I know how hard you people have to work, sweetie."

He felt his blood simmering. "Surely most of us have to work hard, don't we?"

"I suppose so. But you people have to work so much harder for so much less. It is all so unfair." She sighed helplessly.

"Is it really?"

She was surprised at the remark. As surprised as he was. He must correct himself and concentrate. He realised that he was being hard on her. Maybe too hard. She was still young and inexperienced, just out of university and teaching at some 'coloured' school on the Cape Flats. She threw up her arms and twitched two fingers in each hand to show inverted commas whenever she mentioned 'coloured'. It was her over-eager acquiescence that annoyed him. She agreed too soon.

"We all have our work to do," he added half-heartedly.

"I realise that but sometimes I wonder how you people manage it. Your own work during the day, then to crown it all you try to write at night. It must take a lot out of you."

"Don't you also have work to do?"

"I finish teaching at three. I suppose you know I am at a so-called coloured school." He was afraid she was going to twitch her fingers but she did not this time.

"So you finish at three. Does that leave you sufficient time to agonise about harder-working blacks?"

"I'm sure you don't mean that, sweetie."

"No, I don't. No, I suppose not. But I do work hard up to five-thirty daily and half days on Saturdays."

"I think it is fascinating that you can still find time for your reading and writing. Everything about you people fascinates me."

"Do you find oppression fascinating also?" He regretted the tone he was adopting, but couldn't help himself. He had to react or explode. He knew he was hurting her, but did she know? She seemed totally unaware.

"I'm sorry," she said.

"What for?"

"If I offended you."

"You haven't really."

"Then I'm so glad. Well," she laughed self-consciously, "we must all be off. Mervyn wants to go to bed. You quite sure you don't want a lift?"

All he wanted was to get home and sleep. He was very, very tired. And if he missed the Guguletu bus, there was the long walk ahead of him.

"Do come. We don't need to talk if you don't wish to."

Why must she be so insistent? Couldn't she sense his hostility?

"I have to get all the way to Claremont station."

"I stay in Rondebosch near the university. It won't be much out of my way. I can get you there in time for your bus."

"O.K. then, thanks."

She searched for her keys in the darkness outside. He lit a match to help her. She was smaller than he had thought, with pale-blue eyes and stringy hair. He climbed into her mini.

"Don't you want to drive?" she dangled the keys in front of him.

"No," he said almost savagely.

They moved off in silence, then drove through the city centre. Adderley Street wore a deserted look. As they drove along Sir Lowry Road Dambisa felt he ought to break the silence. But what could he say? It was going to be hard work pretending to be sociable.

"Where do you come from originally?" he asked without much enthusiasm. She brightened. She had been waiting for an opening cue. "You'll never guess."

He didn't feel like guessing.

"Vereeniging in the Transvaal," she said triumphantly.

"I forgive you for that."

"Thanks."

He wasn't sure whether she was being sarcastic.

"I am what you might call *'n ware Suid-Afrikaner*. A *boerenooi van die Transvaal*."

"With liberal ideas?"

"Yes, with liberal ideas. I have always been liberal, as you call it, ever since I was a child. It was my father's influence. He taught me to respect all people."

"And now you spread culture non-racially?"

"Really, sweetie . . ."

This galled him. It was the way she said 'sweetie' and constantly repeated it. It had no real meaning for her, merely a word with which to end a sentence. He was sure she called everyone sweetie. A silly affectation.

"Well, sweetie," she repeated, "my background was liberal, whatever that means. Then university really opened my eyes."

"Do you feel sorry for black people?"

"I feel resentment at injustice. If that means feeling sorry, then I suppose I do. I know so little about politics but I am learning all the time from people like you and Mervyn."

"You find politics fascinating?"

This time the barb seemed to have struck home. She winced slightly. There was a long silence as they drove through Salt River.

"I work here," he said to break the tension.

"How gorgeous."

"What?"

"I said, how gorgeous."

Was she being sarcastic? He decided not to reply. This time she broke the ice.

"Have you been writing for a long time?"

"The last few years."

The silence surged back.

"I also sometimes try my hand. I once had a poem in *Varsity*. I must show it to you and see what you think."

They pulled up at a traffic light.

"That building over there belongs to an uncle of mine. He is the director of a clothing factory."

"Hmmm."

"Wonder what he'd say if he saw me driving around with a black."

"Self-conscious about it?"

"Not really. My father wouldn't mind, but I think the rest of the family would."

"Tell me then, why *do* you drive around with blacks?"

"People are people, aren't they?"

"You seem a bit too preoccupied with colour." He half-hoped that he had annoyed her. That she would be angry. She was not.

"I'm so grateful when you tell me this. If I seem a bit preoccupied then I must be more careful about what I say."

He felt helpless. Would nothing annoy her? Was she a punchbag always ready to absorb punishment?

"Let's have some coffee," she said breezily.

"Where on earth?"

"There's a drive-in near Rondebosch."

"Not for us blacks."

"They don't really mind as long as we remain in the car."

"Sure it's all right?"

"Of course it will be all right. How can they mind?"

"And if they do?"

"We'll tell them to go to hell."

All he wanted was for her to get him to Claremont station so that he could catch the Guguletu bus. What the hell was he doing going to have coffee at this time of night with this crazy white woman?

"Two, please," Jenny ordered the black waiter. "Like a hamburger?"

"No, thanks, just coffee. Isn't it rather late?"

"Don't worry. I'll get you home. Two coffees, please."

The waiter seemed uneasy.

"Two coffees, please," she repeated.

"Please, madam; tonight, the boss he is here."

"So what?"

"He says we not allowed to serve him."

"Who?"

"Him. The boss say we must not serve black people."

"Why not?"

Dambisa was in no mood for any confrontation. He could not understand why he had agreed to have coffee in the first place. Get to Claremont as soon as possible and escape from this woman.

"Could I suggest we get away from here?"

"Why should we, sweetie? Let me have two coffees and hurry please. This gentleman has a bus to catch."

"Madam, the boss he is here tonight. He say we can only serve white people."

"Why?"

"I don't know, madam. I do so because the boss he say so."

"Get two coffees please, and leave the boss to me."

Dambisa felt that things were taking a turn he was unhappy about.

"Look here. I don't really want coffee."

"Well, I do. And I insist that they serve you as well. You are my guest."

"Madam, please don't make trouble. The boss he get very angry. He call the police. I'm not allowed to."

"Allowed to serve people?"

"For goodness sake, can't you see it is not his fault? He is only carrying out instructions. Now let's get quietly away and catch that bus."

"I'm not leaving until we are both served."

The waiter shrugged his shoulders and left for the office.

"Come on. This is our chance to get the hell away from here."

"Don't worry. He's only gone to get the coffee."

"Don't go searching for trouble."

"I'm not searching for trouble, sweetie. All I want are two cups of coffee. Now is that wrong?"

"In South Africa, yes."

The manager appeared suddenly as if from nowhere. He was a huge Greek who for the first time in his life realised that he was a white man when he emigrated to South Africa.

"Now what's all the trouble about?" His accent was still very pronounced.

"No trouble at all. I ordered two cups of coffee. One for myself and one for my friend."

"We don't serve natives here."

"How dare you say that?"

"Look miss, get the hell out of here or you make me call the police."

"The damn cheek. You are not even a South African but . . ."

"You make me call the police?"

"You may do as you please. You don't frighten me."

"All right." The Greek shrugged his shoulders and left for his office. Dambisa felt that the situation was now completely out of control.

"I insist that we leave now."

"And I see no reason why we should, sweetie."

"Don't be so damn stupid."

"I'm not being stupid."

"Just forget all this. Let's go."

"If you have no guts, I'm prepared to call his bluff."

He felt like smacking her. How crazy could she get? Guts? This was asking for unnecessary trouble. Better to leave her car and find his own way home. He shouldn't have come in the first place.

The Greek reappeared as suddenly as the first time. "O.K. So I phone them. The police they are coming now. So you want to go to jail?"

"If you don't drive off now, I'm getting out." His hand was on the door.

"You scared?"

"Yes. I have no guts."

"Why don't you listen to your native boy-friend and save plenty trouble? The police they come now now," the Greek sneered.

"All right. I'm leaving. You can wait for your coffee." He was shivering with anger.

"Well, if you insist, we'll go." She put the car into reverse and then with a screech accelerated into the Main Road.

The Greek shook his head uncomprehendingly and then grinned.

Riva

A cold, misty July afternoon about twenty years ago. I first met Riva Lipschitz under the most unusual circumstances. At that time I was a first-year student majoring in English at the university, one of the few 'coloured' students then enrolled at Cape Town. When I first saw her, Riva's age seemed indefinable. Late thirties? Forty perhaps? Certainly more than twenty years older than I was. The place we met in was as unusual as her appearance. The rangers' hut at the top of Table Mountain near the Hely Hutchinson reservoir, three thousand feet above Cape Town.

George, Leonard and I had been climbing all day. George was talkative, an extrovert, given to clowning. Leonard was his exact opposite, shy and introspective. We had gone through high school together but after matriculating they had gone to work while I had won a scholarship which enabled me to proceed to university. We had been climbing without rest all afternoon, scrambling over rugged rocks damp with bracken and heavy with mist. Twice we were lost on the path from India Ravine through Echo Valley. Now soaking wet and tired we were finally in the vicinity of the rangers' hut where we knew we would find shelter and warmth. Some ranger or other would be off duty and keep the fire warm and going. Someone with a sense of humour had called the hut 'At Last'. It couldn't be the rangers for they never spoke English. On the way, we passed the hut belonging to the white Mountain Club; and slightly below that was another hut reserved for members of the 'coloured' Club. I made some remark about the white club house and the fact that prejudice had permeated even to the top of Table Mountain.

"For that matter we would not even be allowed into the so-called Coloured Mountain Club hut," George remarked, serious for once.

"And why not?"

"Because, dear brother, to get in you mustn't only be so-called coloured, you must also be not too so-called coloured. You must have the right complexion, the right sort of hair, the right address and speak the right sort of Walmer Estate or Wynberg English."

"You mean I might not make it?" I said in mock horror.

"I mean exactly that."

I made some rapid calculations. I was dark, had short, curly hair, came from Caledon Street in District Six but spoke English reasonably well. After all I was majoring in it at a white university. What more could anyone require?

"I'm sure that at a pinch I could make it," I teased George. "I speak English beautifully and am educated well beyond my intelligence."

"My dear boy, it won't help. You look far too coloured, University of Cape Town and all. You are far, far too brown. And in addition you have a lousy address."

I collapsed. "You can't hold all that against me."

Leonard grinned. He was not one for saying much.

We trudged on, instinctively skirting both club huts as widely as possible, until we reached 'At Last', which was ten minutes slogging away, just over the next ridge.

A large main room with a very welcome fire going in the cast-iron stove. How the hell did they get that stove up there when our haversacks felt like lead? Running off the main rooms were two tiny bedrooms belonging to each of the rangers. We removed haversacks and sleeping-bags then took off damp boots and stockings. Both rangers were off duty and made room for us at the fire. They were small, wiry Plattelanders; a hard breed of men with wide-eyed, yellow faces, short hair and high cheekbones. They spoke a pleasant, soft, guttural Afrikaans with a distinct Malmesbury brogue, and broke into easy laughter especially when they tried to speak English. The smell of warming bodies filled the room, and steam rose from our wet shirts and shorts. It became uncomfortably hot and I felt sleepy, so decided to retire to one of the bedrooms, crawl

into my bag and read myself to sleep. I lit a lantern and quietly
left the group. George was teasing the rangers and insisting that
they speak English. I was reading a novel about the massacre in
the ravines of Babi Yar, gripping and revolting: a bit out of place
in the unnatural calm at the top of a cold, wet mountain. I was
beginning to doze off comfortably when the main door of the hut
burst open and a blast of cold air swept through the entire place,
almost extinguishing the lantern. Before I could shout anything,
there were loud protests from the main room. The door slammed
shut again and then followed what sounded like a muffled apology.
A long pause, then I made out George saying something. There
was a short snort, followed by peals of loud, uncontrolled laughter.
I felt it was uncanny. The snort, then the rumbling laughter growing in intensity, then stopping abruptly.

By now I was wide awake and curious to know to whom the laugh
belonged, though far too self-conscious to join the group immediately. I strained to hear scraps of conversation. Now and then I
could make out George's voice and the low, soft Afrikaans of the
rangers. There was also another voice which sounded feminine,
but nevertheless harsh and screechy. My curiosity was getting the
better of me. I climbed out of the sleeping-bag and as unobtrusively
as possible joined the group around the fire. The newcomer was
a gaunt, angular white woman, extremely unattractive, looking incongruous in heavy, ill-fitting mountaineering clothes. She was the
centre of the discussion and enjoying it. She was in the middle of
making a point when she spotted me. Her finger remained poised
in mid air.

"And who may I ask is that?" She stared at me. I looked back
into her hard, expressionless grey eyes.

"Will someone answer me?"

"Who?" George asked grinning at my obvious discomfort.

"Him. That's who."

"Oh, him?" George laughed. "He's Paul. He's the greatest literary genius the coloured people have produced this decade. He's written a poem."

"How exciting," she dismissed me. The others laughed. They were obviously under her spell.

"Let me introduce you. This is Professor Paul. First-year Bachelor of Arts. University of Cape Town."

"Cut it out," I said very annoyed at him.

George ignored my remark. "And you are? I have already forgotten."

She made a mock, ludicrous bow. "Riva Lipschitz. Madame Riva Lipschitz. The greatest Jewish watch-repairer and mountaineer in Cape Town. Display shop, 352 Long Street."

"All right, you've made your point. Professor Paul . . . Madame Lipschitz." I mumbled a greeting, keeping well in the background. I was determined not to participate in any conversation. I found George's flattering of her loathsome. The bantering continued, to the amusement of the two rangers. Leonard smiled sympathetically at me. I remained poker-faced waiting for an opportunity when I could slip away. George made some amusing remark (I was not listening) and Riva snorted and began to laugh. So that was where it came from. She saw the look of surprise on my face and stopped abruptly.

"What's wrong, Professor? Don't you like the way I laugh?"

"I'm sorry, I wasn't even thinking of it."

"It makes no difference whether you were or not. Nevertheless I hate being ignored. If the others can treat me with the respect due to me, why can't you? I'm like a queen, am I not, George?" I wasn't sure whether she was serious or not.

"You certainly are like a queen," he laughed.

"Everyone loves me except the Professor. Maybe he thinks too much."

"Maybe he thinks too much of himself," George added.

She snorted and started to laugh at his witticism. George glowed with pride. I took in her ridiculous figure and dress. She was wearing a little knitted skullcap, far too small for her, from which wisps of mousy hair were sticking. A thin face, hard around the mouth, grey eyes, and a large nose I had seen in caricatures of Jews. She seemed flat-chested under her thick jersey which hung down to stick-thin legs stuck into heavy woollen stockings and heavily studded climbing-boots.

"Come on, Paul, be nice to Riva," George encouraged.

"Madame Riva Lipschitz, thank you. Don't you think I look like a queen, Professor?" I maintained my rigid silence.

"Your Professor obviously does not seem over-friendly. Don't you like whites, Professor? I like everyone. I came over specially to be friendly with you people."

"Who are you referring to as you people?" I was getting angry. She seemed temporarily thrown off her guard at my reaction, but immediately controlled herself and broke into a snort.

"The Professor is extremely sensitive. You should have warned me. He doesn't like me but we shall remain friends all the same; won't we, Professor?"

She shot out her hand for me to kiss. I ignored it. She turned back to George and for the rest of her stay pretended I was not present. When everyone was busy talking I slipped out quietly and returned to the bedroom.

Half asleep I could pick up scraps of conversation. George seemed to be explaining away my reaction, playing clown to her queen. Then they forgot all about me. I must have dozed off for I awoke suddenly to find someone shaking my shoulder. It was Leonard.

"Would you like to come with us?"

"Where to?"

"Riva's Mountain Club hut. She's invited us over for coffee, and to meet Simon, whoever he is."

"No, I don't think I'll go."

"You mustn't take her too seriously."

"I don't intend to. Only I don't like her type and the way George is playing up to her. Who the hell does she think she is, after all? What does she want with us?"

"I really don't know. You heard she said she was a watch-repairer somewhere in Long Street. Be reasonable, Paul. She's just trying to be friendly."

"While playing the bloody queen? Who does she think she is because she's white?"

"Don't be like that. Come along with us. She's just another person." George appeared, grinning widely. He attempted an imitation of Riva's snort.

"You coming or not?" he asked, laughing. For that moment I disliked him intensely.

"I'm certainly not." I rolled over in my bag to sleep.

"All right, if that's how you feel."

I heard Riva calling for him, then after a time she shouted. "Goodbye, Professor, see you again some time." Then she snorted and they went laughing out at the door. The rangers were speaking softly and I joined them around the fire, then fell asleep there. I dreamt of Riva striding with heavy, impatient boots and stick-thin legs over mountains of dead bodies in the ravines of Babi Yar. She was snorting and laughing while pushing bodies aside, climbing upwards over dead arms and legs.

It must have been much later when I awoke to the door opening and a stream of cold air rushing into the room. The fire had died down and the rangers were sleeping. George and Leonard were stomping and beating the cold out of their bodies.

"You awake, Paul?" George shouted. Leonard shook me gently.

"What scared you?" George asked, "Why didn't you come and have coffee with the queen of Table Mountain?"

"I can't stand her type. I wonder how you can."

"Come off it, Paul. She's great fun." George attempted a snort and then collapsed with laughter.

"Shut up, you fool. You'll wake the rangers. What the hell did she want here anyway?"

George sat up, tears running down his cheeks. He spluttered and it produced more laughter. "She was just being friendly, dear brother Paul, just being friendly. Fraternal greetings from her Mountain Club."

"Her white Mountain Club?"

"Well, yes, if you put it that way, her white Mountain Club. She could hardly join the so-called coloured one, now, could she? Wrong hair, wrong address, wrong laugh."

"I don't care where she goes as long as you keep her away from me. I have no need to play up to whites and Jews."

"Now really, Paul," George seemed hurt. "Are you anti-Semitic as well as being anti-white?" My remark must have hit home.

"No, I'm only anti-Riva Lipschitz."

"Well, anyhow, I like the way she laughs." He attempted another imitation, but when he started to snort he choked and collapsed to the floor coughing and spluttering. I rolled over in my bag to sleep.

Three months later I was in the vicinity of Upper Long Street. George worked as a clerk at a furniture store in Bree Street. I had been busy with an assignment in the Hiddingh Hall library and had finished earlier than expected. I had not seen him since we had last gone mountaineering, so strolled across to the place where he worked. I wanted to ask about himself, what he had been do-ing since last we met, about Riva. A senior clerk told me that he had not come in that day. I wandered around aimlessly, at a loss what to do next. I peered into second-hand shops without any real interest. It was late afternoon on a dull, overcast day and it was rapidly getting darker with the promise of rain in the air. Upper Long Street and its surrounding lanes seemed more depressing, more beaten up than the rest of the city. Even more so than District Six. Victorian double-storied buildings containing mean shops on the ground floors spilled over into mean side-streets and lanes. To catch a bus home meant walking all the way down to the bottom of Adderley Street. I might as well walk all the way back. Caledon Street, the noise, the dirt, the squalor. My mood was as depressing as my immediate surroundings. I did not wish to stay where I was and at the same time did not wish to go home immediately. What was the number she had said? 352 or 325? I peered through the windows of second-hand bookshops without any wish to go inside and browse. 352, yes that was it. Or 325? In any case I had no money to buy books even if I had the inclination. Had George been at work he might have been able to shake me out of this mood, raise my spirits.

I was now past the swimming-baths. A dirty fly-spotted delicatessen store. There was no number on the door, but the name was boldly displayed. Madeira Fruiterers. Must be run by some homesick Portuguese. Next to it what seemed like a dark and dingy watchmakers. Lipschitz - Master Jewellers. This must be it. I decided to enter. A shabby, squat, balding man adjusted an eyepiece he was wearing and looked up from a workbench cluttered with assorted broken watches.

"Excuse me, are you Mr Lipschitz?" I wondered whether I should add 'Master Jeweller'.

"What exactly do you want?" He had not answered my question. He repeated, "What can I do for you?" His accent was guttural and foreign. I thought of Babi Yar. I was about to apologise and say that I had made some mistake when from the far side of the shop came an unmistakable snort.

"My goodness, if it isn't the Professor!" and then the familiar laugh. Riva came from behind a counter. My eyes had become accustomed to the gloomy interior. The squat man was working from the light filtering in through a dirty window. Rickety showcases and counters cluttered with watches and cheap trinkets. A cat-bin, still wet and smelling pungently, stood against a far counter.

"What brings the Professor here? Coming to visit me?" She nodded to the squat man indicating that all was in order. He had already shoved back his eyepiece and was immersed in his work.

"Come to visit the queen?"

This was absurd, I could not imagine anything less regal, more incongruous. Riva, queen? As gaunt as she had looked in the rangers' hut. Now wearing an unattractive blouse and old-fashioned skirt. Her face as narrow, strained and unattractive as ever. I had to say something, explain my presence.

"I was just passing."

"That's what they all say. George said so last time."

What the hell did that mean? I started to feel uncomfortable. She looked at me coyly. Then she turned to the squat man.

"Simon, I think I'll pack up now. I have a visitor." He showed no sign that he had heard her. She took a shabby coat from a hook.

"Will you be late tonight?" she asked him. Simon grumbled some unintelligible reply. Was this Simon whom George and Leonard had met? Simon the mountaineer? He looked most unlike a mountaineer. Who the hell was he then? Her boss? Husband? Lover? Lipschitz – the Master Jeweller? Or was she Lipschitz, the Master Jeweller? That seemed most unlikely. Riva nodded to me to follow. I did so as there was no alternative. Outside it was dark already.

"I live two blocks down. Come along and have some tea." She did not wait for a reply but began walking briskly, taking long strides. I followed as best I could half a pace behind.

"Walk next to me," she almost commanded. I did so. Why was I going with her? The last thing I wanted was tea.

"Nasty weather," she said, "bad for climbing." Table Mountain was wrapped in a dark mist. It was obviously ridiculous for anyone to climb at five o'clock on a weekday afternoon in heavy weather like this. Nobody would be crazy enough. Except George perhaps.

"George," she said as if reading my thoughts. "George. What was the other one's name?"

"Leonard."

"Oh, yes, Leonard. I haven't seen him since the mountain. How is he getting on?"

I was panting to keep up with her.

"I don't see much of them except when we go climbing together. Leonard works in Epping and George in Bree Street."

"I know about George." How the hell could she?

"I've just come from his work. I wanted to see him but he hasn't come in today."

"Yes, I knew he wouldn't be in. So you came to me instead? I somehow knew that one day you would put in an appearance."

How the hell did she know? Was she in contact with George? Daily contact? I remained quiet, out of breath with the effort of keeping up with her. What on earth made me go into the shop of Lipschitz – Master Jeweller? Who the hell was Lipschitz – Master Jeweller?

The conversation had stopped. She continued the brisk pace, taking her fast, incongruous strides. Like stepping from rock to rock up Blinkwater or Babi Yar.

"Here we are." She stopped abruptly in front of an old triple-storied Victorian building with brown paint peeling off its walls. On the upper floors were wide balconies ringed with wrought-iron railings. The main entrance was cluttered with spilling refuse bins.

"I'm on the first floor."

We mounted a rickety staircase, then came to a landing and a long, dark passage lit at intervals by solitary electric bulbs. All the doors, where these could be made out, looked alike. Riva stopped before one and rummaged in her bag for a key. Next to the door was a cat-litter smelling sharply. The same cat?

"Here we are." She unlocked the door, entered and switched on a light. I was hesitant about following her inside.

"It's quite safe, I won't rape you," she said and snorted. This was a coarse remark. I waited for her to laugh but she did not. I entered, blinking my eyes. A large, high-ceilinged, cavernous bed-sitter with a kitchen and toilet running off it. The room was gloomy and dusty. A double bed, round table, two comfortable-looking chairs and a dressing-table covered with bric-à-brac. There was a heavy smell of mildew permeating everything. The whole building smelt of mildew. Why a double bed? For her alone or Simon and herself?

"You live here?" It was a silly question and I knew it. I wanted to ask, 'You live here alone or does Simon live here also?' Why should I bother about Simon?

"Yes, I live here. Have a seat. The bed's more comfortable to sit on." I chose one of the chairs. It creaked as I settled into it. All the furniture must have been bought from second-hand junk shops. Or maybe it came with the room. Nothing was modern. Jewish-Victorian, or what I imagined Jewish-Victorian to be. Dickensian in a sort of decaying nineteenth-century way. Riva took her coat off. She was all hurry and bustle.

"Let's have some tea. I'll put on the water." Before I could refuse she disappeared into the kitchen. I must leave now. The surroundings were far too depressing. Riva was far too depressing. I remained as if glued to my seat. She reappeared. Now to make my apologies. I spoke as delicately as I could, but it came out all wrongly.

"I'm very sorry, but I won't be able to stay for tea. You see, I really can't stay. I must be home. I have lots of work to do. An exam tomorrow. Social Anthrop."

"The trouble with you, Professor, is that you are far too clever, but not clever enough." She sounded annoyed. "Maybe you work too hard, far too hard. Have some tea before you go." There was a twinkle in her eye again. "Or are you afraid of me?" I held my breath, expecting her to laugh but she did not. A long pause.

"No," I said at last, "No, I'm not afraid of you. I really do have an exam tomorrow. You must believe me. I was on my way home. I was hoping to see George."

"Yes, I know, and he wasn't at work. You've said so before."

"I really must leave now."

"Without first having tea? That would be anti-social. An intellectual like you should know that."

"But I don't want any tea, thanks." The conversation was going around in meaningless circles. Why the hell could I not go if I wished to?"

"You really are afraid of me. I can see that."

"I must go."

"And not have tea with the queen? Is it because I'm white or Jewish? Or because I live in a room like this?"

I wanted to say, 'It's because you're you. Why can't you leave me alone?' I got up determined to leave.

"Why did you come with me in the first place?"

This was an unfair question. I had not asked to come along. There was a hiss from the kitchen where the water was boiling over on the plate.

"I don't know why I came. Maybe it was because you asked me."

"You could have refused."

"I tried to."

"But not hard enough."

"Look, I'm going now. I have overstayed my time."

"Just a second." She disappeared into the kitchen. I could hear her switching off the stove, then the clicking of cups. I stood at the door waiting for her to appear before leaving. She entered with a tray containing the tea things and a plate with some assorted biscuits.

"No, thanks," I said, determined that nothing would keep me. "Said I was leaving and I am."

She put the tray on the table. "All right then, Professor. If you must, then you must. Don't let me keep you any longer." She looked almost pathetic that moment, staring dejectedly at the tray. This was not the Riva I had learnt to know. She was straining to control herself. I felt dirty, sordid, sorry for her.

"Goodbye," I said hastily and hurried out into the passage. As I swiftly ran down the stairs I heard her snorting. A short pause and then peals of uncontrolled laughter. I stumbled into Long Street.

The Visits

It was on the evening The Student had gone out that The Woman had first arrived. It wasn't actually a visit, but that was the nearest he could come to it. He remembered it very clearly. First the phone call for the Student, some girl or other, then the front-door banging. The Student revving his engine and the tortured whine as the Honda gathered speed up the driveway.

He was distinctly annoyed. He went to the front-door, opened it, peered out from long habit, then closed the door gently as if to make up to it for The Student's treatment. He returned to his study and sat down at the cluttered desk. Should he read or mark books? He was busy fighting his way through an anthology of South African verse. What a bore. What a boring bore. Should he mark the Standard Ten compos instead? Mark books?

There was a quietness which settled over the flat. It was like that whenever The Student went out and he took the phone off the cradle. The silence surging softly backwards . . . but first the storm before the calm. The phone, then the revving of that damn engine, then peace. Mark books. Standard Ten compos. Remember, dearest children, the word *can* denotes ability, whereas *may* denotes possibility. Ability and possibility. Can ability. May possibility. Can-ability, may-possibility. He repeated it mentally until a rhythm formed. May-possibility sounded clumsy, so he changed it to canability, mayability. But that was wrong. Sacrificing rhythm for meaning. Maybe he could use it on his seniors. His students. The Student?

He got up, uncomfortable at the triviality of his ideas. Must be getting old. Mr Chips. Old at forty-five. Young at forty-five. He walked to the kitchen to make some tea and turned on the tap for hot water. The gurgle echoed through the flat. How vacant the place sounded without The Student. How empty when he wasn't there. How empty when he was there. A different kind of emptiness.

Impossible to speak to him any longer. He was too . . . too physical. Throwing his weight around and his good looks. Girls, the telephone and the Honda. His unholy trinity. A student of rags and tatters. He switched on the stove reflectively, and put on the water. Mayability, canability. Canability, mayability.

It was then that he heard the knocking at the door. Not loud but it could be heard throughout the flat. Who could it be? He was curious but didn't answer the door at once. He fussed loudly in the kitchen to show that he was in (he knew he could be heard at the entrance) until the knocking was repeated. He coughed and said, "Coming."

When he opened the door he was surprised and disappointed to see the African woman standing there.

"Yes?" he asked, somewhat annoyed.

She said nothing, just stood there, her eyes downcast. He took in her appearance. She was extremely unattractive, seemed all of a heap from her doughy bosom to her thick ankles hanging over her shoes.

"Yes?" he repeated, showing his impatience.

She looked at him for the first time and he noticed a mixture of shyness and aggression. He felt like shutting the door on her, but was incapable of such behaviour. He braced himself and became the teacher. (For God's sake, boy, open your mouth when you recite. Can denotes ability. May possibility.)

Then she said in a half-whisper, "I want food." And as an after-thought, "Please."

It was the way she said it that made him look at her more close-ly. Although she whispered, her tone was not servile or pleading. She spoke almost as if the asking for food was hers by right. Not quite a demand, more a taking for granted. He wanted her to go, but there was something about her he didn't quite understand. He couldn't see her eyes very clearly but sensed they were laughing and mocking him. When he tried to see she cast them down.

"Food?" he repeated, and knew he sounded foolish. She maintained her silence, not looking him in the face.

"Wait here, I'll see." He realised that this was a sign of defeat. But why should he be defeated? There was no contest, or was there?

What he knew was that he had to get away from her. He wished The Student had been there. He could have dealt physically with the situation. But this was so different. He went back to the kitchen and stood for some time staring at the water boiling over on the stove and hissing on the plate. Then he opened the provisions cupboard and started filling an empty carrier-bag. Sugar, rice, a tin of mushrooms. There was some apricot jam left over, a bottle of pickles, stuffed olives. What the hell could she do with stuffed olives? He opened the fridge and removed cheese, butter and two pints of milk. Then he opened the bread tin. He stared at the bulging carrier on the kitchen table.

He seemed afraid to face her and hoped she would be gone by the time he returned to the door. He decided to have a cup of tea while playing for time. Should he invite her in? He smiled and decided against the tea. Then resolutely he took the paper carrier. Give her the food and tell her to get the hell away.

When he handed over the provisions she made a slight, old-fashioned bow. It seemed comical because he estimated she could not be more than forty. Still, one could never tell with these people. Or could one?

"Thank you," she said in the same whisper. Then she was gone. He returned to the kitchen, feeling relieved and, for no reason at all, completely exhausted.

The second time the woman came, it was almost like her first visit. Had she visited him? One did not visit and ask for food. The Student was out again (flexing his muscles at some giddy fresher in a coffee bar). He had been in his study for some time reading the book on South African verse. It wasn't quite as boring as he had thought at first.

Roy Campbell. 'Upon a dark and gloomy night.' Yes it was a dark and gloomy night. Outside it was dark with squalls of north-wester. 'Upon a gloomy night with nobody in sight, I went abroad when all my house was hushed.' To waste the poetry of that great Spanish mystic St John of the Cross upon the snot-nosed brats in his matriculation class. (For goodness sake, try to feel what the poet is trying to get at. Feel the *brio*.) They lived for Hondas and girls and pop. Telephones and screaming singers. The Animals. The Insecticides.

He settled down for more Roy Campbell. 'In safety, in disguise, in darkness up the secret stair I crept . . .' He recognised the knock at once when it came and was afraid to answer.

She stood halfway in the shadow of the entrance but he had no difficulty in recognising the dumpy figure, the heavy legs and the downcast eyes. This time he was determined that she should speak first. She had the empty carrier-bag with her. He did not want to break the silence. Somehow he seemed afraid of his own voice. She held out the bag without saying anything.

"What is it this time?" he demanded in his schoolmaster voice. Then he regretted his tone and felt his attitude was wrong, far too aggressive. There was certainly no cause for aggression.

"More food?" he asked, hoping he sounded friendly.

"Yes, please," she said at last.

He went into the kitchen and half-filled the bag with all the leftovers he could find. By the time he returned he felt more at ease, more in control of himself, and was determined to speak.

"Tell me," he said without handing over the bag, "what is your name? Who are you?"

She mumbled something which sounded like Edith. The surname was inaudible. He didn't bother to ask her to repeat it.

"Now look here, Edith or whoever you are." He spoke faster than usual, his voice a trifle raspy. "Now look here. You're a grown woman. You should be working instead of begging like this. Take the carrier but don't come back here again. Do you understand?"

She nodded slightly and took the food with the same old-fashioned bow. Then, like the first time, she was gone.

He went back to his study and slumped down in the chair. He took up his book but had no further interest in Roy Campbell. Edith something or other. For God's sake why must she come to him? What had he done to her? What had he done for her? He felt guilty but there was nothing he could think of to feel guilty about. He had given her food. He had done his duty. What was his duty and why should he do it? Again the nagging feeling of guilt. Well, he had to tell her not to come again. Couldn't keep giving food away. Not a charitable institution. He wished The Student would come home earlier so that they could talk. No, not about the woman necessarily. Only just talk.

He sat in the dark until well after eleven o'clock when he heard The Student's Honda whining up the driveway. Then he went to bed.

Even after her third visit he said nothing to The Student about it. They seldom spoke, communicating only when necessary. (The Student was in sometimes now because examinations were pressing.) The night of her third visit, however, The Student was out, and he was alone in the flat, although himself on the verge of going out. He was going out more frequently now. He sometimes visited two members of his staff with whom he was quite intimate, and his one married sister. Most times he sat in the public library reading until closing time. He even went to cinemas although he detested them. What he seemed afraid of was being alone in the flat. The loneliness got him down. Or was it aloneness? He used to enjoy it before. The silence, his books, his pipe. A cup of tea

and a small brandy with water before turning in for the night. He couldn't stand the sameness any longer. And the loneliness. One tired of too much routine. And loneliness.

He had put on his overcoat and prepared himself mentally for the brisk walk to the library. The dark shadows of the trees lining the avenue, the smell of rain. He was about to pick up his books when the knock came. He looked around for possible escape routes but there was only the bathroom window and he realised how absurd it was for him to climb through that.

She stood in the doorway holding the same empty carrier.

"But I told you not to come back!" He tried to control himself. "I told you not to come again."

She maintained her silence, her eyes as usual downcast. He clenched the library books till he could feel the edges cutting into his palm.

"Do you understand me?"

She nodded slightly.

"I told you to stay away! Do you understand? Stay away!" She stood dumbly, not looking at him.

"If you come again, I'll be forced to call the police. Police!" he repeated.

She started slightly and cast a quick glance at him. He felt it was hostile.

"Police!" he repeated. "Police!"

There was a pause that lasted longer than it should have done.

"Hell," he said, dropping the books on the table. "Hell, what do I do now?" He decided to try to be reasonable and sat down wearily.

"Where you from?"

She kept her eyes down, not replying.

"Look," he said, "I'll give you food for the last time. For the last time. You understand? You must never come again. If you do come

I'll call the police. Then you'll go to jail! Understand?"

She stared at him, her eyes no longer downcast.

"Jail! Police! Jail!"

Then he noticed, almost with a start, that she was crying. Two tears rolled down her cheeks but her face remained immobile. The tears did not seem part of her. He felt the sense of guilt again. Felt like assuring her that he would not call the police. That he was only pretending. But she must not come again.

He went into the kitchen, and when he returned she took the carrier with the same quaint bow. He watched her walking down the driveway. Then he saw another dark figure joining her. They seemed to speak for a short time, but it was too far for him to hear what they were saying. She pointed at him still standing in the open doorway. The other figure (he could not make out the sex) also turned. He heard their loud laughter. He shut the door and felt sick to the stomach.

She came again the following week and the week after, and every week after that. Now he merely went to the door, took her empty carrier and then filled it. Now no words passed between them, only the ritual. The quaint bow and she was gone. He bought extra groceries which he set aside for her. She did not always come on the same evening, but she never came more than once a week. She seemed to time her visit so that The Student was out and he was in.

Although he watched her when she left, he never saw her companion again. He began suffering from lack of sleep, was short-tempered with his pupils at school and was seriously thinking of giving The Student notice and then himself moving from the flat. There was no one to whom he could speak seriously about the visits.

He told The Student about it one evening but he turned it into a joke and they both laughed. He seemed to welcome and dread her visits at the same time. He wanted to find out more about her, follow her and see where she lived. Was she married? Did she have children? Why did she have to beg? Was it only to him she came? But somehow he was afraid, afraid he might find out. He could ask her in, give her some tea and then ask questions. He was afraid of her answers.

Then one week she did not appear. Her groceries remained in the closet. The following week she did not come either. He kept the groceries (in case). After she had not appeared for a month he decided to use the provisions he had bought for her. With a strange sense of fear he opened the bags and was relieved when nothing happened. He felt as if an enormous burden had dropped from his shoulders and wanted to speak to someone about it. Anyone. The Student was in his room trying in vain to study. He made some coffee and took it to The Student, standing in the doorway attempting to keep the conversation alive.

"By the way," The Student said, not annoyed at being disturbed, "your girlfriend turned up last week but you were out."

"I was out?" he said bewildered. He was eager to know more.

"I answered the door and there she was. What an ugly bitch."

"Yes?" He hoped he had not sounded over-anxious.

"I told her to get away, clear off, hamba!" He waved his arms to indicate the action. "She wouldn't."

"What did you do?" His lips were trembling.

"What you should have done the first time."

"What I should have done?"

"Yes. I took her by her black neck and frog-marched her down the driveway. Then threw her out."

He felt a tightening across his chest. His fists balled and he felt like hitting The Student. He was shivering all over.

"She won't come again," The Student reassured him.

"You shouldn't have done that." He tried to control his voice.

"Why the hell not?" The Student looked at him puzzled.

"You shouldn't have done that," he repeated lamely.

"Are you sick or something?" The Student asked.

"I'm all right. Only have to get back to my books. Marking to be done." The Student looked at him in a strange way. Then the phone rang.

He went into his study and slumped down at the desk. He felt like crying but could not. He heard The Student banging the front-door, then the revving of his Honda engine. Long after the whine had faded away he sat at his desk just staring in the dark.

Make Like Slaves

He certainly felt in no mood for speaking and even his hard guttural yesses and noes cost him an effort. Everything seemed to
depress him: the baleful orange lights over Rosmead Avenue; the
damp, early-evening air whining past the open window of the
Volkswagen; and especially her monotonous voice. He searched
for cigarettes and found the packet empty. Irritably he shoved his
hands into his pockets. She caught the movement and glanced
quickly at him, then concentrated on her driving and talking. Or
talking and driving. She rather liked him and said so. But in a
curious way she was a little afraid of him. She liked the rather heavy
features, the high cheekbones and the grey-green eyes. Could almost
pass. Almost one of us, she thought. Most unfortunate he wasn't.
Would have made things easier. It raised complications to drive
around a coloured male. Coloured male. So-called coloured male.
She mentally played with the words. Capital C or small c? Coloured
gentleman. How did they say again at drama school? Gentleman
of colour. It made complications driving around a gentleman of
colour, no matter how fair. Even with grey-green eyes. More grey
than green. More green than grey. Not safe in Cape Town. Not
safe in all South Africa. Certainly worse in Johannesburg and
Bloemfontein. Possible in London. A so-called gentleman of colour.
But then London was not like Cape Town. Her mind went back
to her student days when she had first gone to Central School, had
first seen Tottenham Court Road and had done her drama course.
She could have remained in England and not come back. She supposed he could also have remained. Had they met there, they might
have become even better friends, although still merely friends. No
more.

"Pull up at the nearest shop, please." His voice had the slightest
touch of command in it. He hoped she had not detected it.

"Excuse me?"

"I wonder whether you could stop at a shop." He mumbled

something about cigarettes. She leaned over breastily and cocked
her ear to hear him above the engine.

"Cigarettes? There are some in the cubby."

He wasn't really sure whether he should smoke, although he felt
like it. Turning he fumbled for them. Cigarettes spilt over him.
She giggled. Jesus, he couldn't bear the way she giggled. Evasively
he began to feel for stray cigarettes. Anything rather than having
to speak or just staring at the road unfolding. Why the hell had
she dragged him out of his flat to go with her to a goddam African
location to see a goddam god-forsaken drama group? What the hell
made him an authority on drama? or Africans?

"Light one for you?" he asked.

"Please." She giggled again. The sound was hard and brittle.

He began to say something, then stopped. He handed her the
lit cigarette and drew deeply at his. Menthol. He disliked menthol
in spite of the advertisements.

"I want you to realise my problem," she said as if there had been
no break in their conversation. "How to get through to them? How
does one communicate across the colour line? How does one over-
come resistance? Hostility? There seems to be hostility," she assured
him. He felt like saying: For God's sake stop acting the bloody
white lady, the grand patroness. Be yourself, dammit, and stop
pretending to bring culture to the poor, starving blacks. They don't
like your culture and your patronisation. They don't like you.

"But they do need me," she said as if reading his mind," and in
a way I need them. I do want to help. I know it sounds sentimen-
tal but I really want to help. It's difficult to interpret their attitude.
You see, they are not what one would call openly hostile. You know
what I mean? They smile; they are pleasant. But I'm aware that
there is an undercurrent. I know they are sneering behind my back.
How does one get across to the African?" She glanced at him for
a moment, then her eyes were back on the road.

He inhaled deeply and blew out smoke in an exaggerated manner. "Why do you smoke menthol?" he asked.

She was not to be put off.

"I wonder how it affects you being neither white nor black? How would you feel in such a situation being a coloured man? Or a gentleman of colour?"

There was a long pause while her question hung in the air. She waited patiently for him to say something.

"I don't know," he said lamely. "I don't really know. I'm not sure what a coloured man is, or – what was it you called me? – a gentleman of colour."

The Volkswagen turned down Wetton Road and picked up speed once it turned into Lansdowne Road.

"Don't you like menthol?" she asked.

"Not really. Please stop at a shop. Must get my own. Can't smoke all of yours."

"Oh, I really don't mind. So you see," she came back to her main topic again," you see it puts me in an invidious position. The Consulate wants me to stage the show in three weeks' time. If it had been the locals wanting it I should have refused. But I can't refuse the Consulate. After what they are doing for their own negroes. Three weeks and we are nowhere near production."

"Your theme seems a bit ambitious."

"I don't really think so. It fits perfectly. The Consulate will love it. It ties up their situation so neatly with ours. A stroke of genius and diplomacy if I may say so." She giggled her hard laugh again. "They'll love it. Negro slavery. My cast won't find it too difficult. Slavery was part of the African experience."

"Now look here . . ." he began slowly and deliberately. She broke in.

"I know The Consulate will love it, and my people are able to do it. There is a close relationship between their experience and that of the American negro."

"*Now look here*," he repeated, allowing her no quarter, "your cast is African, like ourselves. All right they are black Africans, but they are certainly not American negroes. They can't be expected to sing Swing Low and Deep River with conviction. Most American blacks can't do it; it's not part of their experience. So can *your* cast do it?"

He stopped short, realising that his tone was becoming patronising, not only towards her but also towards the Nyanga Players whom he had not yet met. It was a quality he found very annoying in others. Still, her attitude irked him. White produces negro saga with local black talent for foreigners. Coloured pseudo-critic sits in. Or pseudo-coloured critic. Oh, what the hell. Drums and tom-toms and Swing Low. Nyanga's answer to Missa Lubba or Were you there when they crucified My Lord. Why should she pick on him to play the local peacemaker? Trouble with the darkies. Kaffirs are getting cheekier. How did she say it again? Some local theatre slang she had brought back from Central School. Oh yes. Make like slaves. Trouble with the locals. We won't make like slaves. We're tired of making like slaves. Slaves of the theatre world unite. Insurrections and pass burnings. The ride of the Deacons, black Klansmen out of the Locations. Burn black cross burn. Don't make like slaves.

Almost uncannily she replied, "It's because you're coloured that I thought you might get through to them more easily. They might not mind you so much as they do me."

"Maybe," he said, deciding to change the subject but uncertain what to say next. He fumbled in his pocket.

"A shop for cigarettes, please."

"Have another menthol. I've a full packet in my bag. Light one for me as well."

He lit one for her. She took it, noticing that he was not smoking.

"It was an exciting experience when it started. Someone had to step in when Max left, and they were desperately in need of a producer. When The Consulate asked me to put on a show I realised that this was it. What better than the story of slavery? I know my Africans can do it."

He wanted to speak but decided against it. She looked at him quickly.

"You don't seem to agree. Remember, you must tell me the moment I'm wrong. I'm depending on your judgement."

"Sure," he said resignedly.

She continued to build up enthusiasm. "Act One is in Africa. They sing tribal songs. They dance. Palm fronds and the throb of the primitive. You should hear them singing. You should just hear their singing. And the dancing. The most wonderful improvisation."

He found difficulty in analysing his attitude towards her. He couldn't catalogue it in terms of any single emotion. It wasn't love, it wasn't hate. Not contempt, nor antipathy, nor indifference. He didn't know her well enough to have so clear-cut a reaction. A brief meeting on the liner when returning from England. She had seemed as bored as he, bored at the inane deck-games, fancy-dress balls, nautical sports. In his case he was pretending to be bored more than being really so. The only brown face in a shipload of whites. Predominantly white South Africans returning home. Two days before arriving in Cape Town and not a soul had spoken to him. Then she had come to stand at the rail he was leaning against, thrown convention to the wind and started to speak. He mentally classified her as the type of white who shook hands with a black a bit too soon. So they spoke about London and Central School and Hyde Park, and their fellow passengers, and prejudices and South African attitudes. At Cape Town docks they had exchanged addresses and then disembarked. Once home in Claremont he had forgotten all about her. At Christmas she sent him a card, which he strung up with his other cards. Months later she had suddenly appeared. His bed was not made but she flounced down on it prepared to be thrilled at his books, his airport art, his African curios most probably made in Hong Kong; prepared to be thrilled with him. Then she enthusiastically told him about the drama group she was assisting in Nyanga.

"We're all one big family. I love every one of them. I treat them as equals and they in return respect me for that. But when there's work to be done, I'm the boss. Theatre demands discipline. The situation is hierarchical. That's what I was taught and that's what I'm teaching them."

Whining of the Volkswagen engine.

"Stop at the nearest shop, please. I need a cigarette badly." He spoke rather loudly and sensed that he had hurt her. She pulled up the car with a jerk. His tone now was almost apologetic.

"Shall I get some for you?"

"I've got another packet, thanks."

"Good."

The second time she had come to his room she was not quite as enthusiastic about the Nyanga Players. Members of the cast were proving troublesome. Gossiping behind her back; always late for rehearsals; not memorising lines. They could not or would not memorise lines. They were not putting heart and soul into it.

"Couldn't you come and see what's going wrong? If I'm at fault I want you to tell me. They have the potential and talent. But I'm beginning to feel they resent something about me. Not my colour. If it were so I would understand. I know how they suffer. I know how you suffer."

She opened the car door for him as he came out of the shop. He sat down as she started the engine, and lit a cigarette for himself without offering her one. She slipped into low gear and pulled away.

The atmosphere was strained, he could feel it sharply. She hung over the steering-wheel, concentrating a bit too hard on the road. After a few minutes of this he felt compelled to say something.

"Won't there be trouble about my being in the Location without a permit or something?"

"Not really. They don't bother much about it these days. We rehearse at the Community Centre." Her voice sounded matter-of-fact. She was obviously still annoyed.

"You haven't finished," he said trying to make up for his previous attitude.

"Finished what?"

"The slavery story. So it starts in Africa."

"Yes, it starts in Africa. You want to hear more?" She was giving him another chance. "We have tribal singing. The second act is the middle passage. You know, the transport of slaves from Africa to America. They sit chained to the floor and sing their sorrow songs. It's a beautiful part."

He thought of Robert Hayden. Countee Cullen. Yet do I marvel at this curious thing: To make a poet black and bid him sing.

"And then?" he asked, his momentary enthusiasm now completely gone. She noticed this too. She seemed to be paying more attention to him than to herself.

"Sure you want to hear more?"

"Quite sure."

"You seem bored."

He laughed, sounding hollow and unconvincing.

"Well then, the final act is America. They work in the cotton fields. They sing their spirituals. I discovered some lovely poetry I will use in the background. Paul Dunbar, Arna Bontemps, Langston Hughes. Know them?"

"Not really." He thought of Countee Cullen. To make a poet black and bid him sing.

"You should hear my people. If only I could get them to co-operate."

They had by now reached the outskirts of the Location. Sub-economic houses stretched their monotony into the darkness. Streets were badly lit and seemed far too deserted.

"What a shame to live like this," she cried. "No individuality, all houses the same. I feel depressed every time I come here."

"I know that feeling," he said ambiguously. It was the first time he had ever been in a black Location.

"They work under such difficult conditions. They come from their jobs at night, stand in long queues, and then have to come home to this." The Location sprawled away under her indignation. "To this. And then they still have to come to rehearsals. I should really understand."

"What work do they do?" he asked.

"I'm not really sure. Certainly unskilled labour. I only see them at rehearsals, and even then it's difficult to get through to them."

"Throw a party at your home and invite the whole happy lot. Then you can really talk."

She chewed the question. "Yes," she said. Then she continued, "I wonder whether they dislike the part of slaves. It reminds them too much of their past. They most probably equate it with the present."

"Maybe," he said.

"Think so?"

"There's a distinct possibility."

"If it were so I would abandon the play at once. Consulate or no Consulate. But how am I to know unless they tell me? I don't want to hurt them."

"I see," he said.

She pointed out the Community Hall to him. A lonely light flickered in the entrance.

"What's the time?" she asked.

He screwed his eyes but could not see. He lit a match.

"Eight twenty-five."

"We're late but that doesn't matter. They won't be on time either. They never are. Just you wait and see." She made a face at him.

Slowly she manoeuvred the car over a sandpath, then pulled up at the wire gate. Before opening the door she said earnestly, "Now remember, I want you to watch everything, but everything, and tell me afterwards where I go wrong. Don't be afraid to correct me. I want to know if and when I'm to blame."

He followed her into the foyer. From the main hall came the strains of a jazz quartet. Peals of laughter and shuffling feet. They turned left along a passage and entered a small room. Five actors were lounging on benches waiting. She looked at her watch, then nodded knowingly at him. He nodded back slightly.

"Now where are the rest?" she spoke breezily. "Late as usual. Well, we're not waiting for them tonight. We have three weeks left before the show and we can't give up at this late hour. The Consulate expects a show from us and they'll get one."

He sat quietly in a corner seat. The actors stared at her impassively.

"Now then," she said, "where were we last time? Let's start with the third act. I want you to make like slaves."

The Man from the Board

Saturday afternoon in late January. A dull, monotonous, hot and sweaty Saturday afternoon when the knock came at the door of his flat. Rather louder than usual. Isaac sat listlessly at his desk, listless and a trifle irritated at the unexpected interference with his boredom. Three review books for which he had no stomach. The inevitable file of Method assignments for correction. Bored and irritated. A hot Saturday afternoon with nothing he wanted to do. The noon edition of the *Argus* lay half-read, crumpled on the floor. A student's essay lay open on his desk. A dull student's dull essay. Give a detailed analysis of the aims of teaching Oral in the primary school. He wiped a drop of sweat out of his eyes and stared lethargically at the page of scrawled, infantile handwriting. Watch television maybe. Sports. Mediocre club matches, show-jumping, squash. Get into the car and drive anywhere. Why? Where? Where do people always drive to on Saturday afternoons in the heat? Strandfontein? Kalk Bay? Sports meetings? The country? Everyone seems so purposeful, hurrying to so clearly defined a destination. Somewhere definite like out in the country.

The knock came again, louder and slightly more purposeful than the first time.

Cars full of people driving out into the country. A sweaty man with sunglasses, his wife with sunglasses, and a rear-seat full of children and dogs. All looking alike. One can tell the parents by the sunglasses. All determined to get wherever they are determined to get to. And then the stream of returning traffic. Always at six o'clock. Long six-o'clock queues of cars with the same people, the same dogs, the same dogged determination.

The knock again.

Isaac got up, annoyed but a trifle relieved at the temporary respite from boredom. He opened the door slowly, letting in a gust of hot air. He expected to find a hawker or a char looking for work. Instead he found a genial, red, sweaty face grinning at him.

"Yes? What do you want?"

"Are you Mr Jacobs? Mr Isaac Jacobs?"

He took in the figure, straining his eyes against the sunlight. A somewhat dumpy, middle-aged man. A dumpy little man wearing a khaki safari suit. Short, flabby knees, bow legs and long khaki stockings with a black comb stuck in the left one against the calf. What was it Graham had told him? Mike Graham had been with him at Cambridge, and while walking across the lawns of King's had remarked that if a man wore a safari suit with a comb in his sock he was a South African. But if he had no comb he was an Australian and almost sure to be called Neil. All Australians who wore safari suits were called Neil. Graham had made it sound like a great truth.

"Excuse me?" The safari suit opened an official-looking brief case and extracted a cardboard file bursting with papers. He extracted one and ran his finger down a column. "Jacobs, Isaac Vernon?"

"Yes, that's me."

"Sounds Jewish. Ikey Jacobs. You sure you're not Jewish?" his eyes twinkled. "After all, Sammy Davis Junior is Jewish."

Isaac did not find this amusing by any means. It was hot standing in the doorway. Small beads of sweat formed just below his visitor's highly oiled hairline.

"May I come in? The heat's killing me."

"Well, I suppose so. Yes, come inside. But what is it you want?" Isaac felt sure that somewhere his visitor had a Volkswagen Beetle to match his safari suit. A Beetle with a radio and a long aerial with an imitation orange stuck on the tip.

"Actually I'm from the Board." He did not say which Board. "Bredenkamp's the name. Mr Johannes Bredenkamp."

Isaac wasn't sure exactly how his visitor had got inside, but while talking Bredenkamp must have nudged his way past, for the next thing he was sinking down on the couch in the book-filled lounge. He took out an initialled handkerchief and mopped his brow a trifle ostentatiously.

"Nice and cool in here."

Isaac knew it wasn't, but realised that Bredenkamp was determined to make conversation. His annoyance had changed to curiosity. Who was this man? What Board was he from? He seemed to take over the place, to fill the lounge with himself and his handkerchief. Crowding the place with his familiarity.

"Hard work this, working on a hot Saturday afternoon." A pause. Isaac did not know how to respond.

"The Board has tried to contact you on many occasions, Mr . . ."

"Jacobs."

"Mr Jacobs. Didn't you get our circular requesting an interview in our office? We sent the first few by post and then I came myself. I left one here two weeks ago. I put it in your letterbox. Didn't you get it?"

It now made sense. So this was the confrontation. He realised that he had to keep calm. So this was J. M. Bredenkamp whose signature had been below the cyclostyled letter, printed in both official languages on cheap paper, one line of Afrikaans immediately above the translated line in English. Dear Occupier. You are requested to see Mr J. M. Bredenkamp at an address . . . he could not remember. Somewhere in Plein or Barrack Street. Bring along your Identity Card or Book of Life. A request not an order. So he had ignored it. Come and tell Mr J. M. Bredenkamp your race classification. Dear Occupier, what the hell are you doing in the wrong Group Area? Come and show Mr Bredenkamp whether you are qualified or not.

"Did you receive any of our letters?" Bredenkamp's tone was not unpleasant.

"Yes, I received them." His admission sounded flat. Why admit any more and proffer excuses? "Yes, I got your letters."

"Then why didn't you come and see us?" There was still no malice. In fact Bredenkamp clucked as if reprimanding a naughty child.

"Look, Mister. I have a job of work to do. I have students to worry about. I can't just take off every time someone sends me a circular."

"But this is different. This is from the Board."

"So what the hell."

"Mr Jacobs. You realise you are living in a white area."

"Yes?"

"By law you are not allowed to live here. It's illegal."

"Because you people choose to label me coloured?"

"I don't make the laws, Mr Jacobs." Bredenkamp could make a cliché sound even more like a cliché. "I understand exactly how you feel but it's not my business. I'm not responsible for the law. We are only trying to help people like you, Mr Jacobs."

Isaac felt the anger mounting again, but the heat militated against his working up enough enthusiasm. Should he not squash this petty little Napoleon? Hold him responsible? Wipe the grin off his face? The effort would be too much. Or would it?

"We are trying to help you, Mr Jacobs."

"Really? In what way, may I ask?"

"Look at it this way. Wouldn't you be much happier living among your own people?"

Bredenkamp fairly beamed at his solicitousness.

"Now look here . . ."

"Mr Bredenkamp's the name."

"Mr Bredenkamp. Who the hell do you think my people are?"

If the official was aware of any subtlety in the question, any nuance, he showed no sign of it.

"Who the hell are my people?" Isaac repeated.

"The coloured people." Bredenkamp replied promptly.

"Hell. So you've decided to declare me coloured."

"But you are. Aren't you?" Bredenkamp seemed genuinely puzzled at his attitude.

"All right, let's leave it at that for the moment. Now let me ask you a question. Do you sleep well at night?"

"Beg yours?"

"Do you sleep well at night after going around putting people out of their homes?"

"Oh, I see," he beamed, "I see what you are getting at. You are accusing the Board of putting you out of your flat. Do you really believe that, Mr Jacobs?"

"Indeed I do."

"Why do you people always go around accusing us wrongly? Why do you people hate us so? – treat us as if we were Communists or terrorists or such things? We are here to help people like you."

"And you do this by trying to put me out of my flat?"

"Nobody's putting you out. We must obey the law."

"What the hell are you doing here?"

"We are here, Mr Jacobs, I say again, we are here to satisfy people, to help them, to protect them."

"Do I look as if I need your protection?"

"Now come, come, Mr Jacobs. You must be reasonable. Similar people must stay together. Would you like any old skollie to live next door to you?"

Isaac was thrown off his guard for the moment. What exactly did he mean? Was there more in it? Was Bredenkamp hinting that by being in a white area he was the interloper, the skollie? Or was the official genuinely solicitous about who his neighbours should be? Was he as genial and naïve as he pretended to be? Why did he remain so friendly even under provocation? Should he not have jackbooted his way in, barked out a command and demanded that the occupier leave the area or face instant arrest? This man who must have some power (or was he a very petty clerk?) sat and beamed and swallowed insults. Was this the opening gambit of a more serious game? Was Bredenkamp deliberately confusing him? Getting him off his guard? Softening him up?

"What exactly do you mean about skollies living next door to me?"

"I mean what I say. Would you like simply anyone to live next door to you? Any old ruffian? I would certainly object if any white skollie had to come to live next door to me."

"Mr Bredenkamp, I would object to any skollie as my neighbour – whether he is white or black. I insist on the right to choose my neighbours for myself. For instance I might very well object to your living next door to me."

Either Bredenkamp was unaware of the innuendo or chose to ignore it. He did not for a moment lose his composure. Only his left hand in which he kept his crumpled handkerchief kept straying from his brilliantined hair to his brow.

"You don't really mean that, do you?" he asked at last. So he had understood. The barb had driven home.

"No, I don't," Isaac found himself apologising. "No, I don't. I'm sorry. But for goodness sake, Mister, come to the point. What do you want?"

"Anything cool. Have you a fizzy drink or something? Coke or orange will do. Otherwise just a glass of cold water, please."

This deflated Isaac. Was this calculated effrontery, or just sheer ignorance? Or was it a skilful avoidance of unpleasantness? He fetched a glass of orange juice from the fridge in the tiny kitchen. "Sorry, I've run out of Coca-Cola." He must be careful not to appear too friendly. Apologising for his remarks and for the fact that he had no coke. Surely he was at the receiving end? Bredenkamp was there to put him out of his flat. Since when does the victim apologise to the tormentor? This was all wrong.

The official took long sips of the drink, between which he made pleasant clucking noises with his tongue. Then he carefully balanced the half-empty glass on the coffee table and took up his file.

"If you don't mind, now for a little business. Won't keep you long, Mr Jacobs."

"Yes."

"Mind if I ask a few routine questions?"

"Just go ahead."

"Your full name is Isaac Vernon Jacobs?"

"Surely you know that?"

"Race – coloured."

Isaac made no reply.

"Date of birth? Age? Address?"

"Tell me for the umpteenth time. What the hell is this in aid of?"

"Only routine questions, Mr Jacobs, just routine. You don't need to reply if you don't wish to. Job? I suppose you're a teacher or a lecturer."

"Go ahead."

"Where do you teach? University of the Western Cape?" He arched his brows knowingly. Isaac felt glad that Bredenkamp was very wrong but did nothing to disillusion him. Caution. The questions would obviously become less routine, more incriminating. Bredenkamp was no fool. Or was he? The official scribbled almost feverishly. What the hell was he writing?

"Tell me, how did you guess that I was a lecturer at Western Cape?"

"Easy. I can tell by all those books on your shelves."

Could anyone be really so naïve, or was this a very clever act?

"So, if a black man has shelves full of books he must of necessity be a lecturer at Western Cape?"

"Of course." Bredenkamp added with a note of finality. "Besides, you're not black, you're brown."

"Oh, hell. All right, go ahead. Tell me more about myself since you seem to know everything."

"You are obviously a bachelor."

"Spot on. Now how on earth did you know that?" Isaac larded the remarks with heavy sarcasm.

"All those books on your shelves. I told you before."

"I see. Yes indeed. I see. So I am a bachelor because I have books on my shelves. All lecturers at Western Cape are bachelors!"

"I never said that, Mr Jacobs. Besides, I like a man who reads a lot. I'm not a bachelor myself but I like reading. I'm married. Wife and two boys. Johan is seven and Niklaas five. I like my reading. Patience Strong and Zane Grey. You like Patience Strong?"

"Sure. Yes, sure I do."

"And Zane Grey?"

"And Zane Grey."

"Lucky you, being a bachelor and spending most of your time just lecturing and reading."

"I would be far luckier, very much luckier and happier, were you to leave me alone to read in my own flat. Why do you want to put me out of here?"

Bredenkamp looked at him reproachfully. "Now really, Mr Jacobs. I told you before that all we are trying to do is to help you. I'm here for instance to check on Indian businesses in this area. This is a white area. Indians aren't allowed to have businesses here. It's against the law."

"Then why on earth do you have to come to me? Do I look like an Indian business?"

"I know you're not an Indian, Mr Jacobs, you're coloured."

"Oh, hell, not again. If you are searching for Indian businesses, or any other business for that matter, why come to me? Why send me your circulars? Does this flat look like a business to you? Do you find slippers under a bed in a business? Or pots on the stove? Or a television set?"

"I must say you've got a nice set, Mr Jacobs. Sony isn't it? You prefer it?"

"What!"

"You prefer a Sony? I'm thinking about getting one for the boys. I like the colour but my wife is worried about the small screen. Do you find it too small?"

The conversation was becoming Kafkaesque and leading nowhere. Going round in circles. Becoming bizarre.

"Mr Bredenkamp, please listen to me. Could you please finish your questions and leave as soon as possible?"

"Now, now, Mr Jacobs. I'm sorry if I said anything to upset you. I was only talking about the Sony. I'm sorry to take up your time. I also have to earn my living. I really can't understand what you people can have against us."

"I really haven't the time nor the inclination to go into that now. Is there anything else, Mr Bredenkamp? Anything more?"

"Yes, just the last detail. I can come back for the others some other time. What is your annual income? I hope you don't mind my asking?" He sounded apologetic.

"Must I answer that?"

"Not if you don't wish to."

"Then I don't wish to."

Bredenkamp nevertheless seemed to write down an answer. He did some rapid calculations, pursing his lips, then looked up, satisfied. Was he really writing down figures, or information for his superiors? For higher consideration?

"No children of course. Unmarried. You lucky bachelor. You people have all the luck."

Was there a veiled irony in the remark?

Bredenkamp looked Isaac full in the face. It was coming. "Can

I ask you a very important question? It's got nothing to do with the Board." So this was it. This was the showdown.

"Yes?" Isaac braced himself for it.

"What is your philosophy of life?"

Now what the hell did that mean? "Look here, Mister. I've no time for games. If you have relevant questions, ask them."

"This is no game. I'm serious, Mr Jacobs." He looked it.

"All right, Mr Bredenkamp. If I have what you call a philosophy of life, that is my personal affair."

"I know I upset you. I'm sorry. I only ask because I can see from your books that you are a man of education. A man of philosophy. I have two books on philosophy at home. Above my bed. I try to read before I go to sleep but seldom have the time. I'm always busy as you can understand, Mr Jacobs."

"Checking up on Indian businesses?"

"Come, come, Mr Jacobs. You know you're not an Indian."

"Neither am I a bloody business."

Mr Bredenkamp's smile remained but began to look a trifle frayed. Isaac rose to his feet in a manner which made it quite clear that the interview was over.

Bredenkamp sat for a moment, then rose reluctantly.

"Well. That's all for now, Mr Jacobs. You'll be hearing from us soon." He gave no indication whether this was a threat or not. "And thanks for the drink. It was very nice of you." He nudged Isaac playfully in the ribs. "And stick to a Sony. The colour is O.K."

Again Isaac's anger mounted. He steered the official to the door. How did you react towards a man who kept grinning at you? As he opened the door, there was a blast of heat. Bredenkamp stuck out his hand and Isaac reluctantly accepted.

" 'Bye for now. We'll be in contact, Mr Jacobs. I enjoy talking to intellectuals like you. We must have a long chat one day. Next time I come I'll bring my philosophy books with."

It seemed as if he was never going to release Isaac's hand. At length he did.

"Now where did I park my Volksie?"

This was irresistible. Isaac broke into a wide grin for the first time.

"You have a Volksie, Mr Bredenkamp?"

The official nodded while mopping.

"I thought so," said Isaac as he shut his door.

Advance, Retreat

At first the mutterings were only amongst members of the cast but soon the whole of Retreat Senior Secondary School was talking about the autocratic way in which the principal was behaving. He was the one most responsible. How did one deal with such a man, who had had a questionable theatrical career yet insisted on playing Macbeth himself? And who had dragooned the rest of the school into playing all the other roles? Any staff member showing the slightest hint of talent or rebellion had been bullied into the play, to say nothing of senior pupils, who were forced to occupy menial parts such as courtiers, soldiers and Birnam Wood. There was a spirit of rebellion especially among the more radical pupils who were strongly influenced by Macduff, who taught them history. They put up notices about a darkie Shakespeare and a coon Macbeth. Macduff had only recently joined the staff, coming straight out of the University of the Western Cape, sporting a pronounced afro and spouting half-digested Black Identity ideas. He was convinced that it was his destined role to conscientise his pupils and those members of staff prepared to listen to him. He was unhappy about participating in such a play. He would have preferred Ngugi or Soyinka, or even Small or Fugard at a pinch, but Shakespeare! If it hadn't been that this was his first year of teaching and that he had a bullying principal, he would have taken a firm stand. *Macbeth* ran counter to all he stood for. But give the principal enough rope and he would hang himself. Duncan was also not pleased. He was the most senior member of staff in years, having taught English to the principal himself when the latter was writing his Senior Certificate. He was always threatening to reveal the principal's academic record. Now the pupils seemed to single Duncan out for criticism. During every lesson he had to face a barrage of questions from some of Macduff's over-conscientised followers. He would reply with studied superiority.

"I suppose, dearest children, that the production could be seen, even by the likes of you, as a so-called coloured one. *De facto* it could be seen as such. *De jure* it is not. Do you understand the meanings of these subtleties? Don't bother if you don't. In simpler language, it is not our fault that we are seen as a coloured institution. I am using inverted commas. Our task is to prove that in spite of such ethnic labels Shakespeare belongs to all – all except muddle-headed radicals who are long on politics and short on linguistics. I can assure you that if I become convinced that this production of *Macbeth* is in any way a racial one, I shall raise my voice in the appropriate quarters. Now, dearest children, this is my advice to each of you in your hour of intellectual need, 'Plyest thyself to thy books to the end that thou mayest acquire knowledge.' Turn to the 'Intimation Ode' of Wordsworth."

He ignored the catcalls that followed, but felt that the pupils' reaction was not entirely unjustified. There was something wrong with the production. It might be something personal. He knew that *he* should have played Macbeth. He had the talent and experience necessary for the part. Instead he was saddled with Duncan, murdered in Act Two. Last year's production had been even worse. The principal had cast him as Cinna. Not even Cinna the poet (who at least had more speaking lines) but Cinna the conspirator. Senior English teacher, three Unisa courses in English, twenty years of teaching experience in senior secondary schools; and cast as Cinna, the conspirator! At least the role of Duncan was an improvement. Showed that the principal was forced to recognise his talent.

The dress rehearsal was scheduled for six o'clock that night in the school hall. The whole of the morning the pupils seemed more restless than usual, which had given him a bad headache. He might be able to relax at home that afternoon before returning to the school at six. The period just before break he had sat in his office holding his head. There was a loud bang at his door. He looked up, straining through the dull ache, to see Lady Macbeth framed in the entrance, swinging a tennis racquet in her hand. His headache cleared slightly at the sight of her. She was the very ample gym mistress who insisted on wearing very tight tights especially when she knew that he would be around. He didn't mind that. At rehearsals they had their little private game. He would slap her backside and say, "This castle hath a pleasant seat." She loved it. The cast sniggered behind their backs. Now she bounced into his office, her fat face visibly upset.

"Heard the latest news?" she inquired, standing in front of his desk, her arms akimbo.

Duncan had not.

"We're taking the play to another venue."

"So?"

"After we open in our school hall, then – wait for it – after that we move to grander climes. *Macbeth* goes to the Fish Hoek Civic Centre. From the housing schemes to white suburbia. It seems that Retreat is no longer good enough to contain our soaring aspirations."

"Whose idea is this?"

"His. His idea. Old Current Affairs. A little bird told me that there will be an announcement after the dress rehearsal tonight. And we are expected to listen meekly and to comply."

"And what if we don't?"

"Then life can be very miserable at Retreat Senior Secondary School. A thwarted principal can be a very dangerous animal. You follow me?"

"But that means a permit must be applied for. By law there must be a permit to allow coloureds – I'm using inverted commas – to perform in a white area for white audiences. Hell, what happens when the pupils hear about this?"

She slapped her thigh meaningfully with the racquet and for a brief moment Duncan forgot his headache and the drama crisis. Then the interval bell rang.

He got hold of Lennox, Malcolm and the First Witch in a corner of the staffroom. He thought of calling in the Porter as well, but the Porter was suspected of carrying information to the principal. In any case it was known that he drank with his pupils. Macduff could be brought in. He was all right if he would stop beating his Black Identity drum. Given a chance he could become long-winded and ideologically boring to a state of tears. He was not in the staffroom. Malcolm was certain that Macduff was at a meeting of his History Society where, at his, Macduff's, suggestion, they were debating 'The Role of the Black Man in the Frontier Wars of Independence'. Most probably the Porter was also there taking mental notes for his superiors.

"Listen, people," Duncan said conspiratorially, "I hear that old Current Affairs is taking *Macbeth* to the Fish Hoek Civic Centre. It's supposed to be a great secret, but I have my sources. No, not the Porter. He's on the other side. Know what it means going to Fish Hoek? We play under a racial permit."

Lennox was visibly shocked. Duncan continued in a half-whisper, glancing over his shoulder. Everyone else in the staffroom was ignoring them.

"It's bad enough playing in a segregated cast, but playing to a segregated audience?"

"Whose idea is it?" Lennox asked.

"Old Current Affairs himself, and his vice-principal. Banquo's as deeply involved in this as his master."

"What can we do about it?"

"I suggest that we all march into the principal's office right now. What do you say?"

They did not feel it was such a good idea. Macbeth was having his tea. It would serve no purpose their all going in at the same time. In fact it could prove counter-productive. Why not a test case? Duncan could go alone. If he got no satisfaction, then much bigger action. They would all stand together and resign from the play. Duncan did not quite agree but was persuaded to try it out.

Retreat Senior Secondary School was a wind-blown, prefabricated structure put up in the housing scheme. It had suffered heavily during the '76 riots. There were rows of broken windows, peeling walls and plenty of smashed desks. The principal was oblivious to all this. His office had a carpet, heavy orange curtains and soft chairs. On the wall was mounted a giant reproduction of the school badge with its proud motto beneath, 'Advance, Retreat.' Once the final bell rang to end the day, he drove off in his BMW to Fairways and forgot about his ill-kempt, unruly and often malnourished charges. But although Retreat Senior Secondary School was deep in the housing scheme, it had a reputation in one particular field. Through the zeal of its principal it put on an annual Shakespeare, usually the Senior Certificate setwork for that year. The audience would consist of puzzled parents, gawping locals and worried Standard Ten pupils from surrounding schools. The production was also reviewed favourably in the *Cape Times* and pictures appeared in *Rapport Extra*. The principal always played the lead, no matter what the Shakespeare. Fortunately they only produced the Bard. There would have been havoc had the school presented *Saint Joan* or *Major Barbara*. He always involved as many people at the school as possible in the production – 'Total Commitment' as he called it. Teachers and pupils all had to display enthusiastic interest. The secretary usually played a minor part and the caretaker helped with the sets. The parents' committee sold fudge during intervals while the principal signed autographs.

His interest in theatre had stretched over many years. While at the University of Cape Town he had played Curio in *Twelfth Night*.

Admittedly he spoke only two lines and could then go home, but he waited religiously for the final curtain call and took it with the rest. Later he graduated to speaking parts in Eoan Group productions. Now, with a school at his mercy, he produced, directed, organised and took the leading roles, a situation resented by staff members such as Duncan, Lennox and Lady Macbeth. There were rumours that if he could he would have played the tempest in *The Tempest*. He was usually so occupied with other matters during rehearsals that he never had any time to learn his own lines. But this did not upset him in the least, as he had, over the years, developed a healthy contempt for his audience. At a performance a few years before, he had become so confused that he had recited Lady Macbeth's lines. It was a traumatic experience to hear his dark-brown bass thundering out, "I have given suck, and know how tender 'tis to love the babe that milks me." Lady Macbeth had never forgiven him. And Duncan maliciously recalled that awful moment during the previous year's production when, as Brutus, the principal had given the full Mark Antony oration with all stops pulled out, over the body of Caesar. Lennox, who played Antony, had no alternative but to repeat the oration at a much subdued level. The remains of Caesar were subjected twice to the same oration. Mark Antony had never forgiven him.

Long after the lunch break was over, Duncan was still kicking his heels outside the principal's office. The secretary informed him that his headmaster was having tea, and when he was having his tea, no one, but no one, disturbed him. He had long teas. Thus by the time Duncan was told he could enter, he was fuming.

Macbeth looked up. "What can I do for you?" He wiped crumbs off his lip.

"I am indeed terribly sorry to disturb your tea" (he hoped it sounded sarcastic) "but I had to see you on an important matter. It pains me to state that I am not happy about the play. I have reservations about it."

"Well, I have none. What are yours?"

"The pupils, especially my Senior Certificate English class, describe it as an ethnic production."

"Ethnic or ethic?" He roared with laughter, then stopped abrubtly.

"Ethnic. They see it as a so-called coloured production."

"No problem at all. Of course it's ethnic. Or ethic if you like."

"Please be serious, sir. Is it a Black production?"

"Brown to be precise."

"All right, brown. Well, everyone, including myself, is unhappy about this."

"I'm not. Anything else."

"Yes, there *is* something else. Rumour has it that there will be a performance in the Fish Hoek Civic Centre."

"Absolutely correct."

"But Fish Hoek is a declared white area."

"I am fully aware of that."

"But we are not allowed to play there except under permit. With respect, sir, may I ask whether you have applied for a racial permit?"

"Of course not. I wouldn't be so naïve."

"Then who did?"

"I got the vice-principal to do it. If you feel strongly about it, then speak to Banquo. But you need have no worries on that score. We already have the permit. We'll show those whites what Retreat Senior Secondary can do, won't we?"

"In that case, sir, I have no alternative but to hand in my resignation from the play."

"Oh, for one moment I thought you were resigning from the profession. However, I'm not allowing you to resign from the play."

Duncan arched his eyebrows expectantly. Macbeth rose from his seat.

"I'm sacking you from it."

Duncan was too shocked to take his outstretched hand.

"Don't take it too hard. You must realise that I have no alternative but to sack you. Besides your limitations as an actor, which we are both aware of, I cannot allow any member of my cast to mix politics with drama. You may go."

Once Duncan had left, Macbeth stood at the window of his office, a slight grin on his face. Duncan's discomfiture did not particularly disturb him. If Duncan must go, he must go. Theatre was like that. And it would not really be a problem finding a substitute. It was about time that the Porter was promoted. Failing that, the caretaker belonged to the Lavender Hill Gospel Singers so should be able to act. At a pinch he could make a dignified King of Scotland, as long as he kept his mouth shut as long as possible. He might be able to sing, but speaking was not his forte. Fortunately Duncan was stabbed to death in Act Two.

The deposed Duncan left his principal's office shattered. He immediately sought out Lennox and Malcolm and broke the dismal news to them. Both felt that the time was now ripe for confrontation. No later than the dress rehearsal that very evening. Spread the word. Duncan is thrown out. No member of the cast must get into costume. No member of the cast must put on make-up. No rehearsal, but a mass meeting. Spell out our demands.

Lady Macbeth was shocked that Duncan could be treated like a common criminal. Lady Macduff pledged her unqualified support. The First and Second Witches were dependable in a crisis. Macduff would organise the pupils in the cast. It was important at this juncture to ask him to curb his Black enthusiasm. It was just the sort of thing Macbeth would look for. The opposition ranks would be thin. No one would really be loyal to the principal. There was an ineffectual, simpering vice-principal, Banquo. Donalbain was new on the staff, just out of Hewat, with pale knees and frightened to death of controversy. The Porter was an informer; but informers were notoriously unstable. If Macbeth had any information about what was happening, the Porter was the most likely source. If they could get a vote taken, Macbeth would be heavily defeated. But would the principal allow matters to go so far? To be defeated by the democratic processes?

Just before six that evening the cast gathered outside the school hall discussing the latest developments in animated groups. Quite a few pupils who were not in the play were also present. These afrohaired disciples of Macduff were there to give ideological body to the protest. Macbeth had not yet arrived, but then he was always fashionably late and kept everyone else waiting. At six exactly Lennox jumped on a bench and called for silence.

"Ladies and gentlemen. Could I have your attention please? We'll all go inside and take seats. There are certain vital matters we have to discuss before we are prepared to continue with the dress rehearsal, if there is going to be any dress rehearsal this evening or any other evening. So, everyone inside, please!"

Once in the hall, he took his stand on the principal's podium, reserved for assemblies. Next to him sat an aggrieved-looking Duncan. Facing them, to the left, sat most of the anti-Macbeth faction: Malcolm, Lady Macbeth (who kept glancing anxiously at Duncan), Lady Macduff, young Fleance and the First and Second Witches. Sitting uncomfortably opposite them were a nervous Banquo, who kept glancing at the entrance, Donalbain and the Third Witch. The latter was pointedly ignored by the two other witches. Near the door sat a noisy group of History Society members with Macduff in disorganised and vociferous control. The Porter sat amongst them, hiccoughing in an alarming manner and grinning at everybody. Lennox once again called for attention and then went into character.

"Ladies and gentlemen, or should I say fellow actors. I am sure that you are all aware of the latest developments, very serious developments in this play, developments that saw the sacking of a respected senior member of our staff and cast because he had the guts to question what he considered to be irregularities." He pointed dramatically at Duncan next to him. "Here sits a man slaughtered by the vaulting ambition of Macbeth and his lackeys. I am speaking metaphorically. All this man did was to try to get answers to two pertinent questions. The first was whether this was a racial or non-racial *Macbeth*. He received an answer after a fashion. Secondly he wished to know whether the play was to be performed in a white area under a permit; a permit which is the symbol of our oppression and humiliation, which would allow us to caper and perform like coons in front of our oppressors. He received an answer after a fashion. He indicated his dissatisfaction, and because of that was arbitrarily sacked from the play. On behalf of all of us, I wish to say to our comrade, Duncan, we admire your gumption."

Duncan spent the rest of the evening looking like an actor who had gumption. The meeting was opened for discussion. Banquo was forced into putting up a feeble, half-hearted defence. He reminded the meeting how much the principal had done to advance coloured theatre, how successful he had been in bringing Shakespeare to the masses, how the name of Retreat Senior Secondary School had become synonymous with that of the Bard. Then he told the meeting how at great personal risk the principal had invested all the school's funds in the play. This was in spite of the fact that auditors could become sticky and that the authorities frowned on that sort of thing. Lennox was amazed at this revelation. Was Banquo extremely naïve, or was he, in a subtle way, getting his own back on his boss? Was he giving the opposition the fuel they needed? For years he had suffered insult and humiliation at the hands of Macbeth. The Third Witch made a passionate plea for unity and drew an analogy from the play itself. Could one imagine *Macbeth* with only one witch? No, it needed all three. How could one witch be burdened with the responsibility of all the predictions? It was ridiculous. *Ex unitate vires.* The other two witches were not impressed. Lennox hinted that they might be left with only one witch if Macbeth continued on his autocratic way. The play might very well end up not only with a reduced number of witches, but without a Lady Macbeth, without a Fleance, without any dignity, without any integrity. Macbeth might be reduced to chopping off his own arrogant head. He was sure Macduff would refuse to do it. Maybe Banquo would oblige. After all he always obliged his masters. The only problem was that he might have to stand on his own two feet in order to do so. That took gumption.

The meeting was really enjoying itself. At the back the pupils were chanting the school motto of 'Advance, Retreat' over and over again. Macduff rose, his fist in the air, to begin a long dissertation on the role of *meaningful* Blackness in *meaningful* theatre. He was warming up to the introduction when there was a commotion at the door. All heads turned. There stood Macbeth himself, baleful, majestic, defiant, in full costume. His entrance almost seemed stage-managed. There was a deadly silence as he walked down the centre aisle. He indicated to Lennox to leave the podium. This Lennox did almost automatically. Macbeth took up his position. His eyes swept the meeting arrogantly, then he spoke.

"Why are you all not in costume?" he demanded. "That is, all except Duncan?" The latter felt his gumption fast deserting him.

"Will someone say something? If there is nothing to say, then go and get into your costumes. You've wasted enough time as it is."

Banquo rose to go but Lennox stopped him. He had to do something, even if it meant his job as a teacher. Addressing the principal while facing the meeting, Lennox began:

"With respect to you, sir, we are not prepared to continue with any rehearsal unless certain matters are cleared up to our satisfaction. There are questions to which only you can give us the answers."

"Well, then, ask them and get done. We can't waste any time. The caretaker has to leave by ten."

"I will be as brief as possible. Firstly, we wish to know, sir, why our worthy friend, colleague and most talented member of the cast, Duncan, was sacked by you."

"He can't act."

"Is that your only reason?"

"It is reason enough."

"We'll leave it at that for the time being." This did not satisfy Duncan. Lennox continued nevertheless, "Secondly, we are unhappy about this being seen as a so-called coloured show."

"What do you people want, a white show?"

"We want a non-racial show."

"Then bring your own whites, blacks and Indians. I'll be quite happy to replace most of you on grounds of lack of talent. Duncan isn't the only one who can't act."

This was too much. Duncan had to say something or burst. "You speak as if you're the only person with any talent. May I remind you, sir, that when you played Brutus last year, people stopped coming after the third night."

"And if you play Duncan the way you have in rehearsals, people won't come after the opening night. Next objection."

Duncan sat down thoroughly deflated. There was an uncomfortable silence.

"No further objections? Then I suggest that you all get into your costumes."

Banquo rose again to move, trying to egg on Donalbain. Lennox stopped both. "There is one further point," he said, "the question of permits. We object to playing under racial permits."

"So do I. It's not your monopoly to object. I did not apply for one."

"Someone must have. Who did?"

"Him." Macbeth pointed to Banquo, who was too dumbfounded to reply.

"I see," Lennox said lamely. He made a further attempt. "One last question, Mr Principal: where did the money for the production come from?"

For the first time it seemed as if Macbeth had lost his composure. He hesitated for a brief moment, then decided to brazen it out.

"That's not your business."

"It might be the school committee's business. Since you won't tell us, we might ask Banquo. Unless he's responsible for that as well."

"He might very well be."

Banquo was not prepared to take the blame a second time. He was still smarting under the unfair permit accusation. Throwing caution to the wind, he jumped up. His hair was dishevelled and his eyes looked wild. He was breathing rapidly.

"I will tell you. If you wish to know, I will tell you. The principal forced me to apply for a permit. He forced me to do his dirty work. He took money from the school funds to use for the play. All the money. And I hope the committee gets to hear about it. I'm sick and tired of having to take the blame for his machinations."

Macbeth attempted to treat Banquo's outburst with indifference, but there was a nervous twitch around his mouth. Lennox smelt blood.

"Well, then," he began, "having heard that, I will move that we all resign from the play. I also suggest that we list our grievances, especially about the source of money for the production, and send it to the school committee. No performance, no admission takings.

No takings, no money to put back into the school funds. No school funds, very awkward questions. Very awkward inquiries. Inspectors' inquiries. School committee's inquiries. Possible demotions. Very possible dismissals. All those in favour that we resign, please show."

Before a vote could be taken, Macbeth stepped off the podium, raising his hands for silence. He seemed a trifle smaller, a little older, a bit less dignified. He seemed to have lost much of his control. There was a tremor in his voice when he began speaking.

"Colleagues, fellow actors and pupils. I have listened very attentively to all that you had to say. Let me state at once that I do appreciate how you feel. Were I in your position I would possibly feel the same way. I speak now not as your head, not as your principal, but as your equal and friend. Of course I am not inflexible. No man is. I, too, can change. I admit that we used money from the school funds for the production, but it was for your sakes that we did so, for our sakes, for the sake of Retreat Senior Secondary School. If it is not possible to replace the money used in so worthy a cause, there could very well be an inquiry. I am convinced that I can defend my own position, but can I defend Banquo's? Should I defend the vice-principal's? For his sake, then, let us carefully reconsider the position."

Banquo was once again left speechless. His last statements had left him exhausted. He realised that he was party to the money's being used, but it had been at Macbeth's insistence.

The principal himself was now near to tears and kept dabbing at the corner of his eyes with a tissue obtained from Lady Macduff. "I must confess to you now," he continued, "that I was never really serious about Duncan's dismissal. A mature and experienced actor like himself should have known that what I did I did under tremendous stress. As a Christian I know that I must be humble and make allowances, even for his limited talent, but then, are we not all limited in some way or another? If his love of theatre is such that he insists on acting, then who am I to deny him that pleasure?"

Duncan was not at all pleased at the way Macbeth's address was going.

"And about the permit issue. If we cannot play under permit then we will not play under permit. If Fish Hoek means compromising our principles, we'll play right here in Retreat where as coloureds in a coloured area we need apply for no permit. And if any whites or blacks wish to come and see our play, let them bring their own permit."

Macduff also had a suspicion that the address was not going in the right direction. How would he explain this away to his friends in Langa and Guguletu? The Porter attempted a weak cheer but was jabbed in the ribs by pupils on both sides of him. Tears were now coursing down Macbeth's cheeks. Lady Macbeth was crying in sympathy.

"Forgive me when I break down like this. It is only because I feel so strongly for you, my people. To those who accuse Retreat Senior Secondary of racialism, I say, this is not a coloured *Macbeth*, nor a white *Macbeth*," he stared pointedly at Macduff, "nor a black *Macbeth*, but a non-racial *Macbeth*, a non-ethnic *Macbeth*. And a pox on him who says otherwise!"

This climax had a grand ringing tone about it. There was now sustained cheering and the History Society chanted the school motto.

"Finally let me appeal directly to you. Not in order to save myself, not in order to save Banquo, not to save Retreat Senior Secondary School, but in order to save Shakespeare!"

His cheeks were wet. Those in the meeting who were not crying with him were clapping furiously. Many were doing both at the same time. Malcolm jumped up immediately to make his rejuvenation speech. Hoarse with emotion Lennox shouted above the applause:

"I speak for all of us. We stand united behind you. The show must go on. Forward to a non-racial *Macbeth*!"

Macduff wanted the meeting to discuss the role of the Black actor in Black theatre, but his plea was drowned in the general euphoria. Lady Macbeth sat blubbering with emotion in spite of angry glares from Duncan. Lennox had his arms around Macbeth. Then the latter pulled himself up to his full height as his voice boomed out:

"Colleagues, forward to the dressing-room and the castle of Inverness in the spirit of our school motto. Advance, Retreat, Advance!"